Solomon Kan Stories

Robert E. Howard

Red Shadows *(Robert E. Howard)*

I. — THE COMING OF SOLOMON

THE MOONLIGHT shimmered hazily, making silvery mists of illusion among the shadowy trees. A faint breeze whispered down the valley, bearing a shadow that was not of the moon-mist. A faint scent of smoke was apparent.

The man whose long, swinging strides, unhurried yet unswerving, had carried him for many a mile since sunrise, stopped suddenly. A movement in the trees had caught his attention, and he moved silently toward the shadows, a hand resting lightly on the hilt of his long, slim rapier.

Warily he advanced, his eyes striving to pierce the darkness that brooded under the trees. This was a wild and menacing country; death might be lurking under those trees. Then his hand fell away from the hilt and he leaned forward. Death indeed was there, but not in such shape as might cause him fear.

"The fires of Hades!" he murmured. "A girl! What has harmed you, child? Be not afraid of me."

The girl looked up at him, her face like a dim white rose in the dark.

"You—who are—you?" her words came in gasps.

"Naught but a wanderer, a landless man, but a friend to all in need." The gentle voice sounded somehow incongruous, coming from the man.

The girl sought to prop herself up on her elbow, and instantly he knelt and raised her to a sitting position, her head resting against his shoulder. His hand touched her breast and came away red and wet.

"Tell me." His voice was soft, soothing, as one speaks to a babe.

"Le Loup," she gasped, her voice swiftly growing weaker. "He and his men —descended upon our village—a mile up the valley. They robbed —slew—burned—"

"That, then, was the smoke I scented," muttered the man. "Go on, child."

"I ran. He, the Wolf, pursued me—and—caught me—" The words died away in a shuddering silence.

"I understand, child. Then—?"

"Then—he—he—stabbed me—with his dagger —oh, blessed saints!—mercy—"

Suddenly the slim form went limp. The man eased her to the earth, and touched her brow lightly.

"Dead!" he muttered.

Slowly he rose, mechanically wiping his hands upon his cloak. A dark scowl had settled on his somber brow. Yet he made no wild, reckless vow, swore no oath by saints or devils.

"Men shall die for this," he said coldly.

II. — THE LAIR OF THE WOLF

"YOU ARE A FOOL!" The words came in a cold snarl that curdled the hearer's blood.

He who had just been named a fool lowered his eyes sullenly without answer.

"You and all the others I lead!" The speaker leaned forward, his fist pounding emphasis on the rude table between them. He was a tall, rangy-built man, supple as a leopard and with a lean, cruel, predatory face. His eyes danced and glittered with a kind of reckless mockery.

The fellow spoken to replied sullenly, "This Solomon Kane is a demon from Hell, I tell you."

"Faugh! Dolt! He is a man—who will die from a pistol ball or a sword thrust."

"So thought Jean, Juan and La Costa," answered the other grimly. "Where are they? Ask the mountain wolves that tore the flesh from their dead bones. Where does this Kane hide? We have searched the mountains and the valleys for leagues, and we have found no trace. I tell you, Le Loup, he comes up from Hell. I knew no good would come from hanging that friar a moon ago."

The Wolf strummed impatiently upon the table. His keen face, despite lines of wild living and dissipation, was the face of a thinker. The superstitions of his followers affected him not at all.

"Faugh! I say again. The fellow has found some cavern or secret vale of which we do not know where he hides in the day."

"And at night he sallies forth and slays us," gloomily commented the other. "He hunts us down as a wolf hunts deer—by God, Le Loup, you name yourself Wolf but I think you have met at last a fiercer and more crafty wolf than yourself! The first we know of this man is when we find Jean, the most desperate bandit unhung, nailed to a tree with his own dagger through his breast, and the letters S.L.K. carved upon his dead cheeks. Then the Spaniard Juan is struck down, and after we find him he lives long enough to tell us that the slayer is an Englishman, Solomon

Kane, who has sworn to destroy our entire band! What then? La Costa, a swordsman second only to yourself, goes forth swearing to meet this Kane. By the demons of perdition, it seems he met him! For we found his sword-pierced corpse upon a cliff. What now? Are we all to fall before this English fiend?"

"True, our best men have been done to death by him," mused the bandit chief. "Soon the rest return from that little trip to the hermit's; then we shall see. Kane can not hide forever. Then—ha, what was that?"

The two turned swiftly as a shadow fell across the table. Into the entrance of the cave that formed the bandit lair, a man staggered. His eyes were wide and staring; he reeled on buckling legs, and a dark red stain dyed his tunic. He came a few tottering steps forward, then pitched across the table, sliding off onto the floor.

"Hell's devils!" cursed the Wolf, hauling him upright and propping him in a chair. "Where are the rest, curse you?"

"Dead! All dead!"

"How? Satan's curses on you, speak!" The Wolf shook the man savagely, the other bandit gazing on in wide-eyed horror.

"We reached the hermit's hut just as the moon rose," the man muttered. "I stayed outside—to watch—the others went in—to torture the hermit—to make him reveal—the hiding-place—of his gold."

"Yes, yes! Then what?" The Wolf was raging with impatience.

"Then the world turned red—the hut went up in a roar and a red rain flooded the valley—through it I saw—the hermit and a tall man clad all in black—coming from the trees—"

"Solomon Kane!" gasped the bandit. "I knew it! I—"

"Silence, fool!" snarled the chief. "Go on!"

"I fled—Kane pursued—wounded me—but I outran —him—got—here—first—"

The man slumped forward on the table.

"Saints and devils!" raged the Wolf. "What does he look like, this Kane?"

"Like—Satan—"

The voice trailed off in silence. The dead man slid from the table to lie in a red heap upon the floor.

"Like Satan!" babbled the other bandit. "I told you! 'Tis the Horned One himself! I tell you—"

He ceased as a frightened face peered in at the cave entrance.

"Kane?"

"Aye." The Wolf was too much at sea to lie. "Keep close watch, La Mon; in a moment the Rat and I will join you."

The face withdrew and Le Loup turned to the other.

"This ends the band," said he. "You, I, and that thief La Mon are all that are left. What would you suggest?"

The Rat's pallid lips barely formed the word: "Flight!"

"You are right. Let us take the gems and gold from the chests and flee, using the secret passageway."

"And La Mon?"

"He can watch until we are ready to flee. Then—why divide the treasure three ways?"

A faint smile touched the Rat's malevolent features. Then a sudden thought smote him.

"He," indicating the corpse on the floor, "said, 'I got here first.' Does that mean Kane was pursuing him here?" And as the Wolf nodded impatiently the other turned to the chests with chattering haste.

The flickering candle on the rough table lighted up a strange and wild scene. The light, uncertain and dancing, gleamed redly in the slowly widening lake of blood in which the dead man lay; it danced upon the heaps of gems and coins emptied hastily upon the floor from the brass-bound chests that ranged the walls; and it glittered in the eyes of the Wolf with the same gleam which sparkled from his sheathed dagger.

The chests were empty, their treasure lying in a shimmering mass upon the bloodstained floor. The Wolf stopped and listened. Outside was silence. There was no moon, and Le Loup's keen imagination pictured the dark slayer, Solomon Kane, gliding through the blackness, a shadow among shadows. He grinned crookedly; this time the Englishman would be foiled.

"There is a chest yet unopened," said he, pointing.

The Rat, with a muttered exclamation of surprize, bent over the chest indicated. With a single, catlike motion, the Wolf sprang upon him, sheathing his dagger to the hilt in the Rat's back, between the shoulders. The Rat sagged to the floor without a sound.

"Why divide the treasure two ways?" murmured Le Loup, wiping his blade upon the dead man's doublet. "Now for La Mon."

He stepped toward the door, then stopped and shrank back.

At first he thought that it was the shadow of a man who stood in the entrance; then he saw that it was a man himself, though so dark and still he stood that a fantastic semblance of shadow was lent him by the guttering candle.

A tall man, as tall as Le Loup he was, clad in black from head to foot, in plain, close-fitting garments that somehow suited the somber face. Long arms and broad shoulders betokened the swordsman, as plainly as the long rapier in his hand. The features of the man were saturnine and gloomy. A kind of dark pallor lent him a ghostly appearance in the uncertain light, an effect heightened by the satanic darkness of his lowering brows. Eyes, large, deep-set and unblinking, fixed their gaze upon the bandit, and looking into them, Le Loup was unable to decide what color they were. Strangely, the mephistophelean trend of the lower features was offset by a high, broad forehead, though this was partly hidden by a featherless hat.

That forehead marked the dreamer, the idealist, the introvert, just as the eyes and the thin, straight nose betrayed the fanatic. An observer would have been struck by the eyes of the two men who stood there, facing each other. Eyes of both betokened untold deeps of power, but there the resemblance ceased.

The eyes of the bandit were hard, almost opaque, with a curious scintillant shallowness that reflected a thousand changing lights and gleams, like some strange gem; there was mockery in those eyes, cruelty and recklessness.

The eyes of the man in black, on the other hand, deep-set and staring from under prominent brows, were cold but deep; gazing into them, one had the impression of looking into countless fathoms of ice.

Now the eyes clashed, and the Wolf, who was used to being feared, felt a strange coolness on his spine. The sensation was new to him—a new thrill to one who lived for thrills, and he laughed suddenly.

"You are Solomon Kane, I suppose?" he asked, managing to make his question sound politely incurious.

"I am Solomon Kane." The voice was resonant and powerful. "Are you prepared to meet your God?"

"Why, Monsieur," Le Loup answered, bowing, "I assure you I am as ready as I ever will be. I might ask Monsieur the same question."

"No doubt I stated my inquiry wrongly," Kane said grimly. "I will change it: Are you prepared to meet your master, the Devil?"

"As to that, Monsieur"—Le Loup examined his finger nails with elaborate unconcern—"I must say that I can at present render a most satisfactory account to his Horned Excellency, though really I have no intention of so doing—for a while at least."

Le Loup did not wonder as to the fate of La Mon; Kane's presence in the cave was sufficient answer that did not need the trace of blood on his rapier to verify it.

"What I wish to know, Monsieur," said the bandit, "is why in the Devil's name have you harassed my band as you have, and how did you destroy that last set of fools?"

"Your last question is easily answered, sir," Kane replied. "I myself had the tale spread that the hermit possessed a store of gold, knowing that would draw your scum as carrion draws vultures. For days and nights I have watched the hut, and tonight, when I saw your villains coming, I warned the hermit, and together we went among the trees back of the hut. Then, when the rogues were inside, I struck flint and steel to the train I had laid, and flame ran through the trees like a red snake until it reached the powder I had placed beneath the hut floor. Then the hut and thirteen sinners went to Hell in a great roar of flame and smoke. True, one escaped, but him I had slain in the forest had not I stumbled and fallen upon a broken root, which gave him time to elude me."

"Monsieur," said Le Loup with another low bow, "I grant you the admiration I must needs bestow on a brave and shrewd foeman. Yet tell me this: Why have you followed me as a wolf follows deer?"

"Some moons ago," said Kane, his frown becoming more menacing, "you and your fiends raided a small village down the valley. You know the details better than I. There was a girl there, a mere child, who, hoping to escape your lust, fled up the valley; but you, you jackal of Hell, you caught her and left her, violated and dying. I found her there, and above her dead form I made up my mind to hunt you down and kill you."

"H'm," mused the Wolf. "Yes, I remember the wench. Mon Dieu, so the softer sentiments enter into the affair! Monsieur, I had not thought you an amorous man; be not jealous, good fellow, there are many more wenches."

"Le Loup, take care!" Kane exclaimed, a terrible menace in his voice, "I have never yet done a man to death by torture, but by God, sir, you tempt me!"

The tone, and more especially the unexpected oath, coming as it did from Kane, slightly sobered Le Loup; his eyes narrowed and his hand moved toward his rapier. The air was tense for an instant; then the Wolf relaxed elaborately.

"Who was the girl?" he asked idly. "Your wife?"

"I never saw her before," answered Kane.

"Nom d'un nom!" swore the bandit. "What sort of a man are you, Monsieur, who takes up a feud of this sort merely to avenge a wench unknown to you?"

"That, sir, is my own affair; it is sufficient that I do so."

Kane could not have explained, even to himself, nor did he ever seek an explanation within himself. A true fanatic, his promptings were reasons enough for his actions.

"You are right, Monsieur." Le Loup was sparring now for time; casually he edged backward inch by inch, with such consummate acting skill that he aroused no suspicion even in the hawk who watched him. "Monsieur," said he, "possibly you will say that you are merely a noble cavalier, wandering about like a true Galahad, protecting the weaker; but you and I know different. There on the floor is the equivalent to an emperor's ransom. Let us divide it peaceably; then if you like not my company, why— nom d'un nom! —we can go our separate ways."

Kane leaned forward, a terrible brooding threat growing in his cold eyes. He seemed like a great condor about to launch himself upon his victim.

"Sir, do you assume me to be as great a villain as yourself?"

Suddenly Le Loup threw back his head, his eyes dancing and leaping with a wild mockery and a kind of insane recklessness. His shout of laughter sent the echoes flying.

"Gods of Hell! No, you fool, I do not class you with myself! Mon Dieu, Monsieur Kane, you have a task indeed if you intend to avenge all the wenches who have known my favors!"

"Shades of death! Shall I waste time in parleying with this base scoundrel!" Kane snarled in a voice suddenly blood- thirsting, and his lean frame flashed forward like a bent bow suddenly released.

At the same instant Le Loup with a wild laugh bounded backward with a movement as swift as Kane's. His timing was perfect; his back-flung hands struck the table and hurled it aside, plunging the cave into darkness as the candle toppled and went out.

Kane's rapier sang like an arrow in the dark as he thrust blindly and ferociously.

"Adieu, Monsieur Galahad!" The taunt came from somewhere in front of him, but Kane, plunging toward the sound with the savage fury of baffled wrath, caromed against a blank wall that did not yield to his blow. From somewhere seemed to come an echo of a mocking laugh.

Kane whirled, eyes fixed on the dimly outlined entrance, thinking his foe would try to slip past him and out of the cave; but no form bulked there, and when his groping hands found the candle and lighted it, the cave was empty, save for himself and the dead men on the floor.

III. — THE CHANT OF THE DRUMS

ACROSS the dusky waters the whisper came: boom, boom, boom!—a sullen reiteration. Far away and more faintly sounded a whisper of different timbre: thrum, throom, thrum! Back and forth went the vibrations as the throbbing drums spoke to each other. What tales did they carry? What monstrous secrets whispered across the sullen, shadowy reaches of the unmapped jungle?

"This, you are sure, is the bay where the Spanish ship put in?"

"Yes, Senhor; the Negro swears this is the bay where the white man left the ship alone and went into the jungle."

Kane nodded grimly.

"Then put me ashore here, alone. Wait seven days; then if I have not returned and if you have no word of me, set sail wherever you will."

"Yes, Senhor."

The waves slapped lazily against the sides of the boat that carried Kane ashore. The village that he sought was on the river bank but set back from the bay shore, the jungle hiding it from sight of the ship.

Kane had adopted what seemed the most hazardous course, that of going ashore by night, for the reason that he knew, if the man he sought were in the village, he would never reach it by day. As it was, he was taking a most desperate chance in daring the nighttime jungle, but all his life he had been used to taking desperate chances. Now he gambled his life upon the slim chance of gaining the Negro village under cover of darkness and unknown to the villagers.

At the beach he left the boat with a few muttered commands, and as the rowers put back to the ship which lay anchored some distance out in the bay, he turned and engulfed himself in the blackness of the jungle. Sword in one hand, dagger in the other, he stole forward, seeking to keep pointed in the direction from which the drums still muttered and grumbled.

He went with the stealth and easy movement of a leopard, feeling his way cautiously, every nerve alert and straining, but the way was not easy. Vines tripped him and slapped him in the face, impeding his progress; he was forced to grope his way between the huge boles of towering trees, and all through the underbrush about him sounded vague and menacing rustlings and shadows of movement. Thrice his foot touched something that moved beneath it and writhed away, and once he glimpsed the baleful glimmer of feline eyes among the trees. They vanished, however, as he advanced.

Thrum, thrum, thrum, came the ceaseless monotone of the drums: war and death (they said); blood and lust; human sacrifice and human feast! The soul of Africa (said the drums); the spirit of the jungle; the chant of the gods of outer darkness, the gods that roar and gibber, the gods men knew when dawns were young, beast-eyed, gaping-mouthed, huge-bellied, bloody-handed, the Black Gods (sang the drums).

All this and more the drums roared and bellowed to Kane as he worked his way through the forest. Somewhere in his soul a responsive chord was smitten and answered. You too are of the night (sang the drums); there is the strength of darkness, the strength of the primitive in you; come back down the ages; let us teach you, let us teach you (chanted the drums).

Kane stepped out of the thick jungle and came upon a plainly defined trail. Beyond through the trees came the gleam of the village fires, flames glowing through the palisades. Kane walked down the trail swiftly.

He went silently and warily, sword extended in front of him, eyes straining to catch any hint of movement in the darkness ahead, for the trees loomed like sullen giants on each hand; sometimes their great branches intertwined above the trail and he could see only a slight way ahead of him.

Like a dark ghost he moved along the shadowed trail; alertly he stared and harkened; yet no warning came first to him, as a great, vague bulk rose up out of the shadows and struck him down, silently.

IV. — THE BLACK GOD

THRUM, THRUM, THRUM! Somewhere, with deadening monotony, a cadence was repeated, over and over, bearing out the same theme: "Fool—fool— fool!" Now it was far away, now he could stretch out his hand and almost reach it. Now it merged with the throbbing in his head until the two vibrations were as one: "Fool—fool—fool—fool—"

The fogs faded and vanished. Kane sought to raise his hand to his head, but found that he was bound hand and foot. He lay on the floor of a hut— alone? He twisted about to view the place. No, two eyes glimmered at him from the darkness. Now a form took shape, and Kane, still mazed, believed that he looked on the man who had struck him unconscious. Yet no; this man could never strike such a blow. He was lean, withered and wrinkled. The only thing that seemed alive about him were his eyes, and they seemed like the eyes of a snake.

The man squatted on the floor of the hut, near the doorway, naked save for a loin-cloth and the usual paraphernalia of bracelets, anklets and armlets. Weird fetishes of ivory, bone and hide, animal and human, adorned his arms and legs. Suddenly and unexpectedly he spoke in English.

"Ha, you wake, white man? Why you come here, eh?"

Kane asked the inevitable question, following the habit of the Caucasian.

"You speak my language—how is that?"

The black man grinned.

"I slave—long time, me boy. Me, N'Longa, ju-ju man, me, great fetish. No black man like me! You white man, you hunt brother?"

Kane snarled. "I! Brother! I seek a man, yes."

The Negro nodded. "Maybe so you find um, eh?"

"He dies!"

Again the Negro grinned. "Me pow'rful ju-ju man," he announced apropos of nothing. He bent closer. "White man you hunt, eyes like a leopard, eh? Yes? Ha! ha! ha! ha! Listen, white man: man-with-eyes-of-a-leopard, he and Chief Songa make pow'rful palaver; they blood brothers now. Say nothing, I help you; you help me, eh?"

"Why should you help me?" asked Kane suspiciously.

The ju-ju man bent closer and whispered, "White man Songa's right-hand man; Songa more pow'rful than N'Longa. White man mighty ju-ju! N'Longa's white brother kill man—with-eyes- of-a-leopard, be blood brother to N'Longa, N'Longa be more pow'rful than Songa; palaver set."

And like a dusky ghost he floated out of the hut so swiftly that Kane was not sure but that the whole affair was a dream.

Without, Kane could see the flare of fires. The drums were still booming, but close at hand the tones merged and mingled, and the impulse-producing vibrations were lost. All seemed a barbaric clamor without rhyme or reason, yet there was an undertone of mockery there, savage and gloating. "Lies," thought Kane, his mind still swimming, "jungle lies like jungle women that lure a man to his doom."

Two warriors entered the hut—black giants, hideous with paint and armed with crude spears. They lifted the white man and carried him out of the hut. They bore him across an open space, leaned him upright against a post and bound him there. About him, behind him and to the side, a great semicircle of black faces leered and faded in the firelight as the flames leaped and sank. There in front of him loomed a shape hideous and obscene—a black, formless thing, a grotesque parody of the human. Still, brooding, bloodstained, like the formless soul of Africa, the horror, the Black God.

And in front and to each side, upon roughly carven thrones of teakwood, sat two men. He who sat upon the right was a black man, huge, ungainly, a gigantic and unlovely mass of dusky flesh and muscles. Small, hoglike eyes blinked out over sin-marked cheeks; huge, flabby red lips pursed in fleshly haughtiness.

The other—

"Ah, Monsieur, we meet again." The speaker was far from being the debonair villain who had taunted Kane in the cavern among the mountains. His clothes were rags; there were more lines in his face; he had sunk lower in the years that had passed. Yet his eyes still gleamed and danced with their old recklessness and his voice held the same mocking timbre.

"The last time I heard that accursed voice," said Kane calmly, "was in a cave, in darkness, whence you fled like a hunted rat."

"Aye, under different conditions," answered Le Loup imperturbably. "What did you do after blundering about like an elephant in the dark?"

Kane hesitated, then: "I left the mountain—"

"By the front entrance? Yes? I might have known you were too stupid to find the secret door. Hoofs of the Devil, had you thrust against the chest with the golden lock, which stood against the wall, the door had opened to you and revealed the secret passageway through which I went."

"I traced you to the nearest port and there took ship and followed you to Italy, where I found you had gone."

"Aye, by the saints, you nearly cornered me in Florence. Ho! ho! ho! I was climbing through a back window while Monsieur Galahad was battering down the front door of the tavern. And had your horse not gone lame, you would have caught up with me on the road to Rome. Again, the ship on which I left Spain had barely put out to sea when Monsieur Galahad rides up to the wharfs. Why have you followed me like this? I do not understand."

"Because you are a rogue whom it is my destiny to kill," answered Kane coldly. He did not understand. All his life he had roamed about the world aiding the weak and fighting oppression, he neither knew nor questioned why. That was his obsession, his driving force of life. Cruelty and tyranny to the weak sent a red blaze of fury, fierce and lasting, through his soul. When the full flame of his hatred was wakened and loosed, there was no rest for him until his vengeance had been fulfilled to the uttermost. If he thought of it at all, he considered himself a fulfiller of God's judgment, a vessel of wrath to be emptied upon the souls of the unrighteous. Yet in the full sense of the word Solomon Kane was not wholly a Puritan, though he thought of himself as such.

Le Loup shrugged his shoulders. "I could understand had I wronged you personally. Mon Dieu! I, too, would follow an enemy across the world, but, though I would have joyfully slain and robbed you, I never heard of you until you declared war on me."

Kane was silent, his still fury overcoming him. Though he did not realize it, the Wolf was more than merely an enemy to him; the bandit symbolized, to Kane, all the things against which the Puritan had fought all his life: cruelty, outrage, oppression and tyranny.

Le Loup broke in on his vengeful meditations. "What did you do with the treasure, which—gods of Hades!—took me years to accumulate? Devil take it, I had time only to snatch a handful of coins and trinkets as I ran."

"I took such as I needed to hunt you down. The rest I gave to the villages which you had looted."

"Saints and the devil!" swore Le Loup. "Monsieur, you are the greatest fool I have yet met. To throw that vast treasure—by Satan, I rage to think of it in the hands of base peasants, vile villagers! Yet, ho! ho! ho! ho! they will steal, and kill each other for it! That is human nature."

"Yes, damn you!" flamed Kane suddenly, showing that his conscience had not been at rest. "Doubtless they will, being fools. Yet what could I do? Had I left it there, people might have starved and gone naked for lack of it. More, it would have been found, and theft and slaughter would have followed anyway. You are to blame, for had this treasure been left with its rightful owners, no such trouble would have ensued."

The Wolf grinned without reply. Kane not being a profane man, his rare curses had double effect and always startled his hearers, no matter how vicious or hardened they might be.

It was Kane who spoke next. "Why have you fled from me across the world? You do not really fear me."

"No, you are right. Really I do not know; perhaps flight is a habit which is difficult to break. I made my mistake when I did not kill you that night in the mountains. I am sure I could kill you in a fair fight, yet I have never even, ere now, sought to ambush you. Somehow I have not had a liking to meet you, Monsieur—a whim of mine, a mere whim. Then—mon Dieu!—mayhap I have enjoyed a new sensation—and I had thought that I had exhausted the thrills of life. And then, a man must either be the hunter or the hunted. Until now, Monsieur, I was the hunted, but I grew weary of the role—I thought I had thrown you off the trail."

"A Negro slave, brought from this vicinity, told a Portugal ship captain of a white man who landed from a Spanish ship and went into the jungle. I heard of it and hired the ship, paying the captain to bring me here."

"Monsieur, I admire you for your attempt, but you must admire me, too! Alone, I came into this village, and alone among savages and cannibals I—with some slight knowledge of the language learned from a slave aboard ship—I gained the confidence of King Songa and supplanted that mummer, N'Longa. I am a braver man than you, Monsieur, for I had no ship to retreat to, and a ship is waiting for you."

"I admire your courage," said Kane, "but you are content to rule amongst cannibals—you, the blackest soul of them all. I intend to return to my own people when I have slain you."

"Your confidence would be admirable were it not amusing. Ho, Gulka!"

A giant Negro stalked into the space between them. He was the hugest man that Kane had ever seen, though he moved with catlike ease and suppleness. His arms and legs were like trees, and the great, sinuous muscles rippled with each motion. His apelike head was set squarely between gigantic shoulders. His great, dusky hands were like the talons of an ape, and his brow slanted back from above bestial eyes. Flat nose and great, thick red lips completed this picture of primitive, lustful savagery.

"That is Gulka, the gorilla-slayer," said Le Loup. "He it was who lay in wait beside the trail and smote you down. You are like a wolf, yourself, Monsieur Kane, but since your ship hove in sight you have been watched by many eyes, and had you had all the powers of a leopard, you had not seen Gulka nor heard him. He hunts the most terrible and crafty of all beasts, in their native forests, far to the north, the beasts-who-walk-like-men—as that one, whom he slew some days since."

Kane, following Le Loup's fingers, made out a curious, manlike thing, dangling from a roof-pole of a hut. A jagged end thrust through the thing's body held it there. Kane could scarcely distinguish its characteristics by the firelight, but there was a weird, humanlike semblance about the hideous, hairy thing.

"A female gorilla that Gulka slew and brought to the village," said Le Loup.

The giant black slouched close to Kane and stared into the white man's eyes. Kane returned his gaze somberly, and presently the Negro's eyes dropped sullenly and he slouched back a few paces.

The look in the Puritan's grim eyes had pierced the primitive hazes of the gorilla-slayer's soul, and for the first time in his life he felt fear. To throw this off, he tossed a challenging look about; then, with unexpected animalness, he struck his huge chest resoundingly, grinned cavernously and flexed his mighty arms. No one spoke. Primordial bestiality had the stage, and the more highly developed types looked on with various feelings of amusement, tolerance or contempt.

Gulka glanced furtively at Kane to see if the white man was watching him, then with a sudden beastly roar, plunged forward and dragged a man from the semicircle. While the trembling victim screeched for mercy, the giant hurled him upon the crude altar before the shadowy idol. A spear rose and flashed, and the screeching ceased. The Black God looked on, his monstrous features seeming to leer in the flickering firelight. He had drunk; was the Black God pleased with the draft—with the sacrifice?

Gulka stalked back, and stopping before Kane, flourished the bloody spear before the white man's face.

Le Loup laughed. Then suddenly N'Longa appeared. He came from nowhere in particular; suddenly he was standing there, beside the post to which Kane was bound. A lifetime of study of the art of illusion had given the ju-ju man a highly technical knowledge of appearing and disappearing—which after all, consisted only in timing the audience's attention.

He waved Gulka aside with a grand gesture, and the gorilla-man slunk back, apparently to get out of N'Longa's gaze—then with incredible swiftness he turned and struck the ju-ju man a terrific blow upon the side of the head with his open hand. N'Longa went down like a felled ox, and in an instant he had been seized and bound to a post close to Kane. An uncertain murmuring rose from the Negroes, which died out as King Songa stared angrily toward them.

Le Loup leaned back upon his throne and laughed uproariously.

"The trail ends here, Monsieur Galahad. That ancient fool thought I did not know of his plotting! I was hiding outside the hut and heard the interesting conversation you two had. Ha! ha! ha! ha! The Black God must drink, Monsieur, but I have persuaded Songa to have you two burnt; that will be much more enjoyable, though we shall have to forego the usual feast, I fear. For after the fires are lit about your feet the devil himself could not keep your carcasses from becoming charred frames of bone."

Songa shouted something imperiously, and blacks came bearing wood, which they piled about the feet of N'Longa and Kane. The ju-ju man had recovered consciousness, and he now shouted something in his native language. Again the murmuring arose among the shadowy throng. Songa snarled something in reply.

Kane gazed at the scene almost impersonally. Again, somewhere in his soul, dim primal deeps were stirring, age-old thought memories, veiled in the fogs of lost eons. He had been here before, thought Kane; he knew all this of old—the lurid flames beating back the sullen night, the bestial faces leering expectantly, and the god, the Black God, there in the shadows! Always the Black God, brooding back in the shadows. He had known the shouts, the frenzied chant of the worshipers, back there in the gray dawn of the world, the speech of the bellowing drums, the singing priests, the repellent, inflaming, all-pervading scent of freshly spilt blood. All this have I known, somewhere, sometime, thought Kane; now I am the main actor—

He became aware that someone was speaking to him through the roar of the drums; he had not realized that the drums had begun to boom again. The speaker was N'Longa:

"Me pow'rful ju-ju man! Watch now: I work mighty magic. Songa!" His voice rose in a screech that drowned out the wildly clamoring drums.

Songa grinned at the words N'Longa screamed at him. The chant of the drums now had dropped to a low, sinister monotone and Kane plainly heard Le Loup when he spoke:

"N'Longa says that he will now work that magic which it is death to speak, even. Never before has it been worked in the sight of living men; it is the nameless ju-ju magic. Watch closely, Monsieur; possibly we shall be further amused." The Wolf laughed lightly and sardonically.

A black man stooped, applying a torch to the wood about Kane's feet. Tiny jets of flame began to leap up and catch. Another bent to do the same with N'Longa, then hesitated. The ju-ju man sagged in his bonds; his head drooped upon his chest. He seemed dying.

Le Loup leaned forward, cursing, "Feet of the Devil! Is the scoundrel about to cheat us of our pleasure of seeing him writhe in the flames?"

The warrior gingerly touched the wizard and said something in his own language.

Le Loup laughed: "He died of fright. A great wizard, by the—"

His voice trailed off suddenly. The drums stopped as if the drummers had fallen dead simultaneously. Silence dropped like a fog upon the village and in the stillness Kane heard only the sharp crackle of the flames whose heat he was beginning to feel.

All eyes were turned upon the dead man upon the altar, for the corpse had begun to move!

First a twitching of a hand, then an aimless motion of an arm, a motion which gradually spread over the body and limbs. Slowly, with blind, uncertain gestures, the dead man turned upon his side, the trailing limbs found the earth. Then, horribly like something being born, like some frightful reptilian thing bursting the shell of non-existence, the corpse tottered and reared upright, standing on legs wide apart and stiffly braced, arms still making useless, infantile motions. Utter silence, save somewhere a man's quick breath sounded loud in the stillness.

Kane stared, for the first time in his life smitten speechless and thoughtless. To his Puritan mind this was Satan's hand manifested.

Le Loup sat on his throne, eyes wide and staring, hand still half-raised in the careless gesture he was making when frozen into silence by the unbelievable sight. Songa sat beside him, mouth and eyes wide open, fingers making curious jerky motions upon the carved arms of the throne.

Now the corpse was upright, swaying on stiltlike legs, body tilting far back until the sightless eyes seemed to stare straight into the red moon that was just rising over the black jungle. The thing tottered uncertainly in a wide, erratic half- circle, arms flung out grotesquely as if in balance, then swayed about to face the two thrones—and the Black God. A burning twig at Kane's feet cracked like the crash of a cannon in the tense silence. The horror thrust forth a black foot—it took a wavering step— another. Then with stiff, jerky and automatonlike steps, legs straddled far apart, the dead man came toward the two who sat in speechless horror to each side of the Black God.

"Ah-h-h!" from somewhere came the explosive sigh, from that shadowy semicircle where crouched the terror-fascinated worshipers. Straight on stalked the grim specter. Now it was within three strides of the thrones, and Le Loup, faced by fear for the first time in his bloody life, cringed back in his chair; while Songa, with a superhuman effort breaking the chains of horror that held him helpless, shattered the night with a wild scream and, springing to his feet, lifted a spear, shrieking and gibbering in wild menace. Then as the ghastly thing halted not its frightful advance, he hurled the spear with all the power of his great, black muscles, and the spear tore through the dead man's breast with a rending of flesh and bone. Not an instant halted the thing —for the dead die not—and Songa the king stood frozen, arms outstretched as if to fend off the terror.

An instant they stood so, leaping firelight and eery moonlight etching the scene forever in the minds of the beholders. The changeless staring eyes of the corpse looked full into the bulging eyes of Songa, where were reflected all the hells of horror. Then with a jerky motion the arms of the thing went out and up. The dead hands fell on Songa's shoulders. At the first touch, the king seemed to shrink and shrivel, and with a scream that was to haunt the dreams of every watcher through all the rest of time, Songa crumpled and fell, and the dead man reeled stiffly and fell with him. Motionless lay the two at the feet of the Black God, and to Kane's dazed mind it seemed that the idol's great, inhuman eyes were fixed upon them with terrible, still laughter.

At the instant of the king's fall, a great shout went up from the blacks, and Kane, with a clarity lent his subconscious mind by the depths of his hate, looked for Le Loup and saw him spring from his throne and vanish in the darkness. Then vision was blurred by a rush of black figures who swept into the space before the god. Feet knocked aside the blazing brands whose heat Kane had forgotten, and dusky hands freed him; others loosed the wizard's body and laid it upon the earth. Kane dimly understood that the blacks believed this thing to be the work of N'Longa, and that they connected the vengeance of the wizard with himself. He bent, laid a hand on the ju-ju man's shoulder. No doubt of it: he was dead, the flesh was already cold. He glanced at the other corpses. Songa was dead, too, and the thing that had slain him lay now without movement.

Kane started to rise, then halted. Was he dreaming, or did he really feel a sudden warmth in the dead flesh he touched? Mind reeling, he again bent over the wizard's body, and slowly he felt warmness steal over the limbs and the blood begin to flow sluggishly through the veins again.

Then N'Longa opened his eyes and stared up into Kane's, with the blank expression of a new-born babe. Kane watched, flesh crawling, and saw the knowing, reptilian glitter come back, saw the wizard's thick lips part in a wide grin. N'Longa sat up, and a strange chant arose from the Negroes.

Kane looked about. The blacks were all kneeling, swaying their bodies to and fro, and in their shouts Kane caught the word, "N'Longa!" repeated over and over in a kind of fearsomely ecstatic refrain of terror and worship. As the wizard rose, they all fell prostrate.

N'Longa nodded, as if in satisfaction.

"Great ju-ju—great fetish, me!" he announced to Kane. "You see? My ghost go out—kill Songa—come back to me! Great magic! Great fetish, me!"

Kane glanced at the Black God looming back in the shadows, at N'Longa, who now flung out his arms toward the idol as if in invocation.

I am everlasting (Kane thought the Black God said); I drink, no matter who rules; chiefs, slayers, wizards, they pass like the ghosts of dead men through the gray jungle; I stand, I rule; I am the soul of the jungle (said the Black God).

Suddenly Kane came back from the illusory mists in which he had been wandering. "The white man! Which way did he flee?"

N'Longa shouted something. A score of dusky hands pointed; from somewhere Kane's rapier was thrust out to him. The fogs faded and vanished; again he was the avenger, the scourge of the unrighteous; with the sudden volcanic speed of a tiger he snatched the sword and was gone.

V. — THE END OF THE RED TRAIL

LIMBS AND VINES slapped against Kane's face. The oppressive steam of the tropic night rose like mist about him. The moon, now floating high above the jungle, limned the black shadows in its white glow and patterned the jungle floor in grotesque designs. Kane knew not if the man he sought was ahead of him, but broken limbs and trampled underbrush showed that some man had gone that way, some man who fled in haste, nor halted to pick his way. Kane followed these signs unswervingly. Believing in the justice of his vengeance, he did not doubt that the dim beings who rule men's destinies would finally bring him face to face with Le Loup.

Behind him the drums boomed and muttered. What a tale they had to tell this night of the triumph of N'Longa, the death of the black king, the overthrow of the white-man-with-eyes-like-a-leopard, and a more darksome tale, a tale to be whispered in low, muttering vibrations: the nameless ju-ju.

Was he dreaming? Kane wondered as he hurried on. Was all this part of some foul magic? He had seen a dead man rise and slay and die again; he had seen a man die and come to life again. Did N'Longa in truth send his ghost, his soul, his life essence forth into the void, dominating a corpse to do his will? Aye, N'Longa died a real death there, bound to the torture stake, and he who lay dead on the altar rose and did as N'Longa would have done had he been free. Then, the unseen force animating the dead man fading, N'Longa had lived again.

Yes, Kane thought, he must admit it as a fact. Somewhere in the darksome reaches of jungle and river, N'Longa had stumbled upon the Secret—the Secret of controlling life and death, of overcoming the shackles and limitations of the flesh. How had this dark wisdom, born in the black and blood-stained shadows of this grim land, been given to the wizard? What sacrifice had been so pleasing to the Black Gods, what ritual so monstrous, as to make them give up the knowledge of this magic? And what thoughtless, timeless journeys had N'Longa taken, when he chose to send his ego, his ghost, through the far, misty countries, reached only by death?

There is wisdom in the shadows (brooded the drums), wisdom and magic; go into the darkness for wisdom; ancient magic shuns the light; we remember the lost ages (whispered the drums), ere man became wise and foolish; we remember the beast gods—the serpent gods and the ape gods and the nameless, the Black Gods, they who drank blood and whose voices roared through the shadowy hills, who feasted and lusted. The secrets of life and of death are theirs; we remember, we remember (sang the drums).

Kane heard them as he hastened on. The tale they told to the feathered black warriors farther up the river, he could not translate; but they spoke to him in their own way, and that language was deeper, more basic.

The moon, high in the dark blue skies, lighted his way and gave him a clear vision as he came out at last into a glade and saw Le Loup standing there. The Wolf's naked blade was a long gleam of silver in the moon, and he stood with shoulders thrown back, the old, defiant smile still on his face.

"A long trail, Monsieur," said he. "It began in the mountains of France; it ends in an African jungle. I have wearied of the game at last, Monsieur—and you die. I had not fled from the village, even, save that—I admit it freely—that damnable witchcraft of N'Longa's shook my nerves. More, I saw that the whole tribe would turn against me."

Kane advanced warily, wondering what dim, forgotten tinge of chivalry in the bandit's soul had caused him thus to take his chance in the open. He half-suspected treachery, but his keen eyes could detect no shadow of movement in the jungle on either side of the glade.

"Monsieur, on guard!" Le Loup's voice was crisp. "Time that we ended this fool's dance about the world. Here we are alone."

The men were now within reach of each other, and Le Loup, in the midst of his sentence, suddenly plunged forward with the speed of light, thrusting viciously. A slower man had died there, but Kane parried and sent his own blade in a silver streak that slit Le Loup's tunic as the Wolf bounded backward. Le Loup admitted the failure of his trick with a wild laugh and came in with the breath-taking speed and fury of a tiger, his blade making a white fan of steel about him.

Rapier clashed on rapier as the two swordsmen fought. They were fire and ice opposed. Le Loup fought wildly but craftily, leaving no openings, taking advantage of every opportunity. He was a living flame, bounding back, leaping in, feinting, thrusting, warding, striking—laughing like a wild man, taunting and cursing.

Kane's skill was cold, calculating, scintillant. He made no waste movement, no motion not absolutely necessary. He seemed to devote more time and effort toward defense than did Le Loup, yet there was no hesitancy in his attack, and when he thrust, his blade shot out with the speed of a striking snake.

There was little to choose between the men as to height, strength and reach. Le Loup was the swifter by a scant, flashing margin, but Kane's skill reached a finer point of perfection. The Wolf's fencing was fiery, dynamic, like the blast from a furnace. Kane was more steady—less the instinctive, more the thinking fighter, though he, too, was a born slayer, with the coordination that only a natural fighter possessed.

Thrust, parry, a feint, a sudden whirl of blades—

"Ha!" the Wolf sent up a shout of ferocious laughter as the blood started from a cut on Kane's cheek. As if the sight drove him to further fury, he attacked like the beast men named him. Kane was forced back before that blood-lusting onslaught, but the Puritan's expression did not alter.

Minutes flew by; the clang and clash of steel did not diminish. Now they stood squarely in the center of the glade, Le Loup untouched, Kane's garments red with the blood that oozed from wounds on cheek, breast, arm and thigh. The Wolf grinned savagely and mockingly in the moonlight, but he had begun to doubt.

His breath came hissing fast and his arm began to weary; who was this man of steel and ice who never seemed to weaken? Le Loup knew that the wounds he had inflicted on Kane were not deep, but even so, the steady flow of blood should have sapped some of the man's strength and speed by this time. But if Kane felt the ebb of his powers, it did not show. His brooding countenance did not change in expression, and he pressed the fight with as much cold fury as at the beginning.

Le Loup felt his might fading, and with one last desperate effort he rallied all his fury and strength into a single plunge. A sudden, unexpected attack too wild and swift for the eye to follow, a dynamic burst of speed and fury no man could have withstood, and Solomon Kane reeled for the first time as he felt cold steel tear through his body. He reeled back, and Le Loup, with a wild shout, plunged after him, his reddened sword free, a gasping taunt on his lips.

Kane's sword, backed by the force of desperation, met Le Loup's in midair; met, held and wrenched. The Wolf's yell of triumph died on his lips as his sword flew singing from his hand.

For a fleeting instant he stopped short, arms flung wide as a crucifix, and Kane heard his wild, mocking laughter peal forth for the last time, as the Englishman's rapier made a silver line in the moonlight.

Far away came the mutter of the drums. Kane mechanically cleansed his sword on his tattered garments. The trail ended here, and Kane was conscious of a strange feeling of futility. He always felt that, after he had killed a foe. Somehow it always seemed that no real good had been wrought; as if the foe had, after all, escaped his just vengeance.

With a shrug of his shoulders Kane turned his attention to his bodily needs. Now that the heat of battle had passed, he began to feel weak and faint from the loss of blood. That last thrust had been close; had he not managed to avoid its full point by a twist of his body, the blade had transfixed him. As it was, the sword had struck glancingly, plowed along his ribs and sunk deep in the muscles beneath the shoulder blade, inflicting a long, shallow wound.

Kane looked about him and saw that a small stream trickled through the glade at the far side. Here he made the only mistake of that kind that he ever made in his entire life. Mayhap he was dizzy from loss of blood and still mazed from the weird happenings of the night; be that as it may, he laid down his rapier and crossed, weaponless, to the stream. There he laved his wounds and bandaged them as best he could, with strips torn from his clothing.

Then he rose and was about to retrace his steps when a motion among the trees on the side of the glade where he first entered, caught his eye. A huge figure stepped out of the jungle, and Kane saw, and recognized, his doom. The man was Gulka, the gorilla-slayer. Kane remembered that he had not seen the black among those doing homage to N'Longa. How could he know the craft and hatred in that dusky, slanting skull that had led the Negro, escaping the vengeance of his tribesmen, to trail down the only man he had ever feared? The Black God had been kind to his neophyte; had led him upon his victim helpless and unarmed. Now Gulka could kill his man openly—and slowly, as a leopard kills, not smiting him down from ambush as he had planned, silently and suddenly.

A wide grin split the Negro's face, and he moistened his lips. Kane, watching him, was coldly and deliberately weighing his chances. Gulka had already spied the rapiers. He was closer to them than was Kane. The Englishman knew that there was no chance of his winning in a sudden race for the swords.

A slow, deadly rage surged in him—the fury of helplessness. The blood churned in his temples and his eyes smoldered with a terrible light as he eyed the Negro. His fingers spread and closed like claws. They were strong, those hands; men had died in their clutch. Even Gulka's huge black column of a neck might break like a rotten branch between them—a wave of weakness made the futility of these thoughts apparent to an extent that needed not the verification of the moonlight glimmering from the spear in Gulka's black hand. Kane could not even have fled had he wished—and he had never fled from a single foe.

The gorilla-slayer moved out into the glade. Massive, terrible, he was the personification of the primitive, the Stone Age. His mouth yawned in a red cavern of a grin; he bore himself with the haughty arrogance of savage might.

Kane tensed himself for the struggle that could end but one way. He strove to rally his waning forces. Useless; he had lost too much blood. At least he would meet his death on his feet, and somehow he stiffened his buckling knees and held himself erect, though the glade shimmered before him in uncertain waves and the moonlight seemed to have become a red fog through which he dimly glimpsed the approaching black man.

Kane stooped, though the effort nearly pitched him on his face; he dipped water in his cupped hands and dashed it into his face. This revived him, and he straightened, hoping that Gulka would charge and get it over with before his weakness crumpled him to the earth.

Gulka was now about the center of the glade, moving with the slow, easy stride of a great cat stalking a victim. He was not at all in a hurry to consummate his purpose. He wanted to toy with his victim, to see fear come into those grim eyes which had looked him down, even when the possessor of those eyes had been bound to the death stake. He wanted to slay, at last, slowly, glutting his tigerish blood-lust and torture-lust to the fullest extent.

Then suddenly he halted, turned swiftly, facing another side of the glade. Kane, wondering, followed his glance.

At first it seemed like a blacker shadow among the jungle shadows. At first there was no motion, no sound, but Kane instinctively knew that some terrible menace lurked there in the darkness that masked and merged the silent trees. A sullen horror brooded there, and Kane felt as if, from that monstrous shadow, inhuman eyes seared his very soul. Yet simultaneously there came the fantastic sensation that these eyes were not directed on him. He looked at the gorilla-slayer.

The black man had apparently forgotten him; he stood, half-crouching, spear lifted, eyes fixed upon that clump of blackness. Kane looked again. Now there was motion in the shadows; they merged fantastically and moved out into the glade, much as Gulka had done. Kane blinked: was this the illusion that precedes death? The shape he looked upon was such as he had visioned dimly in wild nightmares, when the wings of sleep bore him back through lost ages.

He thought at first it was some blasphemous mockery of a man, for it went erect and was tall as a tall man. But it was inhumanly broad and thick, and its gigantic arms hung nearly to its misshapen feet. Then the moonlight smote full upon its bestial face, and Kane's mazed mind thought that the thing was the Black God coming out of the shadows, animated and blood-lusting. Then he saw that it was covered with hair, and he remembered the manlike thing dangling from the roof-pole in the native village. He looked at Gulka.

The Negro was facing the gorilla, spear at the charge. He was not afraid, but his sluggish mind was wondering over the miracle that brought this beast so far from his native jungles.

The mighty ape came out into the moonlight and there was a terrible majesty about his movements. He was nearer Kane than Gulka but he did not seem to be aware of the white man. His small, blazing eyes were fixed on the black man with terrible intensity. He advanced with a curious swaying stride.

Far away the drums whispered through the night, like an accompaniment to this grim Stone Age drama. The savage crouched in the middle of the glade, but the primordial came out of the jungle with eyes bloodshot and blood-lusting. The Negro was face to face with a thing more primitive than he. Again ghosts of memories whispered to Kane: you have seen such sights before (they murmured), back in the dim days, the dawn days, when beast and beast-man battled for supremacy.

Gulka moved away from the ape in a half-circle, crouching, spear ready. With all his craft he was seeking to trick the gorilla, to make a swift kill, for he had never before met such a monster as this, and though he did not fear, he had begun to doubt. The ape made no attempt to stalk or circle; he strode straight forward toward Gulka.

The black man who faced him and the white man who watched could not know the brutish love, the brutish hate that had driven the monster down from the low, forest-covered hills of the north to follow for leagues the trail of him who was the scourge of his kind—the slayer of his mate, whose body now hung from the roof-pole of the Negro village.

The end came swiftly, almost like a sudden gesture. They were close, now, beast and beast-man; and suddenly, with an earth-shaking roar, the gorilla charged. A great hairy arm smote aside the thrusting spear, and the ape closed with the Negro. There was a shattering sound as of many branches breaking simultaneously, and Gulka slumped silently to the earth, to lie with arms, legs and body flung in strange, unnatural positions. The ape towered an instant above him, like a statue of the primordial triumphant.

Far away Kane heard the drums murmur. The soul of the jungle, the soul of the jungle: this phrase surged through his mind with monotonous reiteration.

The three who had stood in power before the Black God that night, where were they? Back in the village where the drums rustled lay Songa—King Songa, once lord of life and death, now a shriveled corpse with a face set in a mask of horror. Stretched on his back in the middle of the glade lay he whom Kane had followed many a league by land and sea. And Gulka the gorilla-slayer lay at the feet of his killer, broken at last by the savagery which had made him a true son of this grim land which had at last overwhelmed him.

Yet the Black God still reigned, thought Kane dizzily, brooding back in the shadows of this dark country, bestial, blood-lusting, caring naught who lived or died, so that he drank.

Kane watched the mighty ape, wondering how long it would be before the huge simian spied and charged him. But the gorilla gave no evidence of having even seen him. Some dim impulse of vengeance yet unglutted prompting him, he bent and raised the Negro. Then he slouched toward the jungle, Gulka's limbs trailing limply and grotesquely. As he reached the trees, the ape halted, whirling the giant form high in the air with seemingly no effort, and dashed the dead man up among the branches. There was a rending sound as a broken projecting limb tore through the body hurled so powerfully against it, and the dead gorilla-slayer dangled there hideously.

A moment the clear moon limned the great ape in its glimmer, as he stood silently gazing up at his victim; then like a dark shadow he melted noiselessly into the jungle.

Kane walked slowly to the middle of the glade and took up his rapier. The blood had ceased to flow from his wounds, and some of his strength was returning, enough, at least, for him to reach the coast where his ship awaited him. He halted at the edge of the glade for a backward glance at Le Loup's upturned face and still form, white in the moonlight, and at the dark shadow among the trees that was Gulka, left by some bestial whim, hanging as the she-gorilla hung in the village.

Afar the drums muttered: "The wisdom of our land is ancient; the wisdom of our land is dark; whom we serve, we destroy. Flee if you would live, but you will never forget our chant. Never, never," sang the drums.

Kane turned to the trail which led to the beach and the ship waiting there.

Skulls in the Stars *(Robert E. Howard)*

CHAPTER ONE

There are two roads to Torkertown. One, the shorter and more direct route, leads across a barren upland moor, and the other, which is much longer, winds its tortuous way in and out among the hummocks and quagmires of the swamps, skirting the low hills to the east. It was a dangerous and tedious trail; so Solomon Kane halted in amazement when a breathless youth from the village he had just left, overtook him and implored him for God's sake to take the swamp road.

"The swamp road!" Kane stared at the boy. He was a tall, gaunt man, was Solomon Kane, his darkly pallid face and deep brooding eyes, made more sombre by the drab Puritanical garb he affected.

"Yes, sir, 'tis far safer," the youngster answered to his surprised exclamation.

"Then the moor road must be haunted by Satan himself, for your townsmen warned me against traversing the other."

"Because of the quagmires, sir, that you might not see in the dark. You had better return to the village and continue your journey in the morning, sir."

"Taking the swamp road?"

"Yes, sir."

Kane shrugged his shoulders and shook his head.

"The moon rises almost as soon as twilight dies. By its light I can reach Torkertown in a few hours, across the moor."

"Sir, you had better not. No one ever goes that way. There are no houses at all upon the moor, while in the swamp there is the house of old Ezra who lives there all alone since his maniac cousin, Gideon, wandered off and died in the swamp and was never found—and old Ezra though a miser would not refuse you lodging should you decide to stop until morning. Since you must go, you had better go the swamp road."

Kane eyed the boy piercingly. The lad squirmed and shuffled his feet.

"Since this moor road is so dour to wayfarers," said the Puritan, "why did not the villagers tell me the whole tale, instead of vague mouthings?"

"Men like not to talk of it, sir. We hoped that you would take the swamp road after the men advised you to, but when we watched and saw that you turned not at the forks, they sent me to run after you and beg you to reconsider."

"Name of the Devil!" exclaimed Kane sharply, the unaccustomed oath showing his irritation; "the swamp road and the moor road—what is it that threatens me and why should I go miles out of my way and risk the bogs and mires?"

"Sir," said the boy, dropping his voice and drawing closer, "we be simple villagers who like not to talk of such things lest foul fortune befall us, but the moor road is a way accurst and hath not been traversed by any of the countryside for a year or more. It is death to walk those moors by night, as hath been found by some score of unfortunates. Some foul horror haunts the way and claims men for his victims."

"So? And what is this thing like?"

"No man knows. None has ever seen it and lived, but late-farers have heard terrible laughter far out on the fen and men have heard the horrid shrieks of its victims. Sir, in God's name return to the village, there pass the night, and tomorrow take the swamp trail to Torkertown."

Far back in Kane's gloomy eyes a scintillant light had begun to glimmer, like a witch's torch glinting under fathoms of cold grey ice. His blood quickened. Adventure! The lure of life-risk and drama! Not that Kane recognized his sensations as such. He sincerely considered that he voiced his real feelings when he said:

"These things be deeds of some power of evil. The lords of darkness have laid a curse upon the country. A strong man is needed to combat Satan and his might. Therefore I go, who have defied him many a time."

"Sir," the boy began, then closed his mouth as he saw the futility of argument. He only added, "The corpses of the victims are bruised and torn, sir."

He stood there at the crossroads, sighing regretfully as he watched the tall, rangy figure swinging up the road that led toward the moors.

The sun was setting as Kane came over the brow of the low hill which debouched into the upland fen. Huge and blood-red it sank down behind the sullen horizon of the moors, seeming to touch the rank grass with fire; so for a moment the watcher seemed to be gazing out across a sea of blood. Then the dark shadows came gliding from the east, the western blaze faded, and Solomon Kane struck out, boldly in the gathering darkness.

The road was dim from disuse but was clearly defined. Kane went swiftly but warily, sword and pistols at hand. Stars blinked out and night winds whispered among the grass like weeping spectres. The moon began to rise, lean and haggard, like a skull among the stars.

Then suddenly Kane stopped short. From somewhere in front of him sounded a strange and eery echo—or something like an echo. Again, this time louder. Kane started forward again. Were his senses deceiving him? No!

Far out, there pealed a whisper of frightful laughter. And again, closer this time. No human being ever laughed like that—there was no mirth in it, only hatred and horror and soul-destroying terror. Kane halted. He was not afraid, but for the second he was almost unnerved. Then, stabbing through that awesome laughter, came the sound of a scream that was undoubtedly human. Kane started forward, increasing his gait. He cursed the illusive lights and flickering shadows which veiled the moor in the rising moon and made accurate sight impossible. The laughter continued, growing louder, as did the screams. Then sounded faintly the drum of frantic human feet. Kane broke into a run. Some human was being hunted to death out there on the fen, and by what manner of horror God only knew. The sound of the flying feet halted abruptly and the screaming rose unbearably, mingled with other sounds unnameable and hideous. Evidently the man had been overtaken, and Kane, his flesh crawling, visualized some ghastly fiend of the darkness crouching on the back of its victim, crouching and tearing. Then the noise of a terrible and short struggle came clearly through the abysmal silence of the night and the footfalls began again, but stumbling and uneven. The screaming continued, but with a gasping gurgle. The sweat stood cold on Kane's forehead and body. This was heaping horror on horror in an intolerable manner. God, for a moment's clear light! The frightful drama was being enacted within a very short distance of him, to judge by the ease with which the sounds reached him. But this hellish half-light veiled all in shifting shadows, so that the moors appeared a haze of blurred illusions, and stunted trees and bushes seemed like giants.

Kane shouted, striving to increase the speed of his advance. The shrieks of the unknown broke into a hideous shrill squealing; again there was the sound of a struggle, and then from the shadows of the tall grass a thing came reeling —a thing that had once been a man—a gore-covered, frightful thing that fell at Kane's feet and writhed and grovelled and raised its terrible face to the rising moon, and gibbered and yammered, and fell down again and died in its own blood.

The moon was up now and the light was better. Kane bent above the body, which lay stark in its unnameable mutilation, and he shuddered, a rare thing for him, who had seen the deeds of the Spanish Inquisition and the witch- finders.

Some wayfarer, he supposed. Then like a hand of ice on his spine he was aware that he was not alone. He looked up, his cold eyes piercing the shadows whence the dead man had staggered. He saw nothing, but he knew—he felt —that other eyes gave back his stare, terrible eyes not of this earth. He straightened and drew a pistol, waiting. The moonlight spread like a lake of pale blood over the moor, and trees and grasses took on their proper sizes. The shadows melted, and Kane saw! At first he thought it only a shadow of mist, a wisp of moor fog that swayed in the tall grass before him. He gazed. More illusion, he thought. Then the thing began to take on shape, vague and indistinct. Two hideous eyes flamed at him—eyes which held all the stark horror which has been the heritage of man since the fearful dawn ages —eyes frightful and insane, with an insanity transcending earthly insanity. The form of the thing was misty and vague, a brain-shattering travesty on the human form, like, yet horribly unlike. The grass and bushes beyond showed clearly through it.

Kane felt the blood pound in his temples, yet he was as cold as ice. How such an unstable being as that which wavered before him could harm a man in a physical way was more than he could understand, yet the red horror at his feet gave mute testimony that the fiend could act with terrible material effect.

Of one thing Kane was sure; there would be no hunting of him across the dreary moors, no screaming and fleeing to be dragged down again and again. If he must die he would die in his tracks, his wounds in front.

Now a vague and grisly mouth gaped wide and the demoniac laughter again shrieked out, soul-shaking in its nearness. And in the midst of that threat of doom, Kane deliberately levelled his long pistol and fired. A maniacal yell of rage and mockery answered the report, and the thing came at him like a flying sheet of smoke, long shadowy arms stretched to drag him down.

Kane, moving with the dynamic speed of a famished wolf, fired the second pistol with as little effect, snatched his long rapier from its sheath and thrust into the centre of the misty attacker. The blade sang as it passed clear through, encountering no solid resistance, and Kane felt icy fingers grip his limbs, bestial talons tear his garments and the skin beneath,

He dropped the useless sword and sought to grapple with his foe. It was like fighting a floating mist, a flying shadow armed with daggerlike claws. His savage blows met empty air, his leanly mighty arms, in whose grasp strong men had died, swept nothingness and clutched emptiness. Naught was solid or real save the flaying, apelike fingers with their crooked talons, and the crazy eyes which burned into the shuddering depths of his soul.

Kane realized that he was in a desperate plight indeed. Already his garments hung in tatters and he bled from a score of deep wounds. But he never flinched, and the thought of flight never entered his mind. He had never fled from a single foe, and had the thought occurred to him he would have flushed with shame.

He saw no help for it now, but that his form should lie there beside the fragments of the other victim, but the thought held no terrors for him. His only wish was to give as good an account of himself as possible before the end came, and if he could, to inflict some damage on his unearthly foe. There above the dead man's torn body, man fought with demon under the pale light of the rising moon, with all the advantages with the demon, save one. And that one was enough to overcome the others. For if abstract hate may bring into material substance a ghostly thing, may not courage, equally abstract, form a concrete weapon to combat that ghost? Kane fought with his arms and his feet and his hands, and he was aware at last that the ghost began to give back before him, and the fearful laughter changed to screams of baffled fury. For man's only weapon is courage that flinches not from the gates of Hell itself, and against such not even the legions of Hell can stand. Of this Kane knew nothing; he only knew that the talons which tore and rended him seemed to grow weaker and wavering, that a wild light grew and grew in the horrible eyes. And reeling and gasping, he rushed in, grappled the thing at last and threw it, and as they tumbled about on the moor and it writhed and lapped his limbs like a serpent of smoke, his flesh crawled and his hair stood on end, for he began to understand its gibbering. He did not hear and comprehend as a man hears and comprehends the speech of a man, but the frightful secrets it imparted in whisperings and yammerings and screaming silences sank fingers of ice into his soul, and he knew.

CHAPTER TWO

The hut of old Ezra the miser stood by the road in the midst of the swamp, half screened by the sullen trees which grew about it. The walls were rotting, the roof crumbling, and great pallid and green fungus-monsters clung to it and writhed about the doors and windows, as if seeking to peer within. The trees leaned above it and their grey branches intertwined so that it crouched in semi-darkness like a monstrous dwarf over whose shoulder ogres leer.

The road, which wound down into the swamp among rotting stumps and rank hummocks and scummy, snake-haunted pools and bogs, crawled past the hut. Many people passed that way these days, but few saw old Ezra, save a glimpse of a yellow face, peering through the fungus-screened windows, itself like an ugly fungus.

Old Ezra the miser partook much of the quality of the swamp, for he was gnarled and bent and sullen; his fingers were like clutching parasitic plants and his locks hung like drab moss above eyes trained to the murk of the swamplands. His eyes were like a dead man's, yet hinted of depths abysmal and loathsome as the dead lakes of the swamplands.

These eyes gleamed now at the man who stood in front of his hut. This man was tall and gaunt and dark, his face was haggard and claw-marked, and he was bandaged of arm and leg. Somewhat behind this man stood a number of villagers.

"You are Ezra of the swamp road?"

"Aye, and what want ye of me?"

"Where is your cousin Gideon, the maniac youth who abode with you?"

"Gideon?"

"Aye."

"He wandered away into the swamp and never came back. No doubt he lost his way and was set upon by wolves or died in a quagmire or was struck by an adder."

"How long ago?"

"Over a year."

"Aye. Hark ye, Ezra the miser. Soon after your cousin's disappearance, a countryman, coming home across the moors, was set upon by some unknown fiend and torn to pieces, and thereafter it became death to cross those moors. First men of the countryside, then strangers who wandered over the fen, fell to the clutches of the thing. Many men have died, since the first one.

"Last night I crossed the moors, and heard the flight and pursuing of another victim, a stranger who knew not the evil of the moors. Ezra the miser, it was a fearful thing, for the wretch twice broke from the fiend, terribly wounded, and each time the demon caught and dragged him down again. And at last he fell dead at my very feet, done to death in a manner that would freeze the statue of a saint."

The villagers moved restlessly and murmured fearfully to each other, and old Ezra's eyes shifted furtively. Yet the sombre expression of Solomon Kane never altered, and his condor-like stare seemed to transfix the miser.

"Aye, aye!" muttered old Ezra hurriedly; "a bad thing, a bad thing! Yet why do you tell this thing to me?"

"Aye, a sad thing. Harken further, Ezra. The fiend came out of the shadows and I fought with it over the body of its victim. Aye, how I overcame it, I know not, for the battle was hard and long but the powers of good and light were on my side, which are mightier than the powers of Hell.

"At the last I was stronger, and it broke from me and fled, and I followed to no avail. Yet before it fled it whispered to me a monstrous truth."

Old Ezra started, stared wildly, seemed to shrink into himself.

"Nay, why tell me this?" he muttered.

"I returned to the village and told my tale," said Kane, "for I knew that now I had the power to rid the moors of its curse forever. Ezra, come with us!"

"Where?" gasped the miser.

"To the rotting oak on the moors." Ezra reeled as though struck; he screamed incoherently and turned to flee.

On the instant, at Kane's sharp order, two brawny villagers sprang forward and seized the miser. They twisted the dagger from his withered hand, and pinioned his arms, shuddering as their fingers encountered his clammy flesh.

Kane motioned them to follow, and turning strode up the trail, followed by the villagers, who found their strength taxed to the utmost in their task of bearing their prisoner along. Through the swamp they went and out, taking a little-used trail which led up over the low hills and out on the moors.

The sun was sliding down the horizon and old Ezra stared at it with bulging eyes—stared as if he could not gaze enough. Far out on the moors reared up the great oak tree, like a gibbet, now only a decaying shell. There Solomon Kane halted.

Old Ezra writhed in his captor's grasp and made inarticulate noises.

"Over a year ago," said Solomon Kane, "you, fearing that your insane cousin Gideon would tell men of your cruelties to him, brought him away from the swamp by the very trail by which we came, and murdered him here in the night."

Ezra cringed and snarled.

"You cannot prove this lie !"

Kane spoke a few words to an agile villager. The youth clambered up the rotting bole of the tree and from a crevice, high up, dragged something that fell with a clatter at the feet of the miser. Ezra went limp with a terrible shriek.

The object was a man's skeleton, the skull cleft.

"You—how knew you this? You are Satan!" gibbered old Ezra.

Kane folded his arms.

"The thing I fought last night told me this thing as we reeled in battle, and I followed it to this tree. For the fiend is Gideon's ghost."

Ezra shrieked again and fought savagely.

"You knew," said Kane sombrely, "you knew what thing did these deeds. You feared the ghost of the maniac, and that is why you chose to leave his body on the fen instead of concealing it in the swamp. For you knew the ghost would haunt the place of his death. He was insane in life, and in death he did not know where to find his slayer; else he had come to you in your hut. He hates no man but you, but his mazed spirit cannot tell one man from another, and he slays all, lest he let his killer escape. Yet he will know you and rest in peace, forever after. Hate hath made of his ghost a solid thing that can rend and slay, and though he feared you terribly in life, in death he fears you not at all."

Kane halted. He glanced at the sun.

"All this I had from Gideon's ghost, in his yammerings and his whisperings and his shrieking silences. Naught but your death will lay that ghost."

Ezra listened in breathless silence and Kane pronounced the words of his doom.

"A hard thing it is," said Kane sombrely, "to sentence a man to death in cold blood and in such a manner as I have in mind, but you must die that others may live—and God knoweth you deserve death.

"You shall not die by noose, bullet or sword, but at the talons of him you slew—for naught else will satiate him."

At these words Ezra's brain shattered, his knees gave way and he fell grovelling and screaming for death, begging them to burn him at the stake, to flay him alive. Kane's face was set like death, and the villagers, the fear rousing their cruelty, bound the screeching wretch to the oak tree, and one of them bade him make his peace with God. But Ezra made no answer, shrieking in a high shrill voice with unbearable monotony. Then the villager would have struck the miser across the face, but Kane stayed him.

"Let him make his peace with Satan, whom he is more like to meet, " said the Puritan grimly. "The sun is about to set. Loose his cords so that he may work loose by dark, since it is better to meet death free and unshackled than bound like a sacrifice." As they turned to leave him, old Ezra yammered and gibbered unhuman sounds and then fell silent, staring at the sun with terrible intensity.

They walked away across the fen, and Kane flung a last look at the grotesque form bound to the tree, seeming in the uncertain light like a great fungus growing to the bole. And suddenly the miser screamed hideously:

"Death! Death! There are skulls in the Stars!"

"Life was good to him, though he was gnarled and churlish and evil," Kane sighed. "Mayhap God has a place for such souls where fire and sacrifice may cleanse them of their dross as fire cleans the forest of fungus things. Yet my heart is heavy within me."

"Nay, sir," one of the villagers spoke, "you have done but the will of God, and good alone shall come of this night's deed."

"Nay," answered Kane heavily. "I know not—I know not." The sun had gone down and night spread with amazing swiftness, as if great shadows came rushing down from unknown voids to cloak the world with hurrying darkness. Through the thick night came a weird echo, and the men halted and looked back the way they had come.

Nothing could be seen. The moor was an ocean of shadows and the tall grass about them bent in long waves before the faint wind, breaking the deathly stillness with breathless murmurings.

Then far away the red disk of the moon rose over the fen, and for an instant a grim silhouette was etched blackly against it. A shape came flying across the face of the moon—a bent, grotesque thing whose feet seemed scarcely to touch the earth; and close behind came a thing like a flying shadow —a nameless, shapeless horror.

A moment the racing twain stood out boldly against the moon; then they merged into one unnameable, formless mass, and vanished in the shadows.

Far across the fen sounded a single shriek of terrible laughter.

Rattle of Bones (Robert E. Howard)

"Landlord, Ho!" The shout broke the lowering silence and reverberated through the black forest with sinister echoing.

"This place hath a forbidding aspect, meseemeth."

Two men stood in front of the forest tavern. The building was low, long and rambling, built of heavy logs. Its small windows were heavily barred and the door was closed. Above the door its sinister sign showed faintly—a cleft skull.

This door swung slowly open and a bearded face peered out. The owner of the face stepped back and motioned his guests to enter—with a grudging gesture it seemed. A candle gleamed on a table; a flame smoldered in the fireplace.

"Your names?"

"Solomon Kane," said the taller man briefly.

"Gaston l'Armon," the other spoke curtly. "But what is that to you?"

"Strangers are few in the Black Forest," grunted the host, "bandits many. Sit at yonder table and I will bring food."

The two men sat down, with the bearing of men who have traveled far. One was a tall gaunt man, clad in a featherless hat and somber black garments, which set off the dark pallor of his forbidding face. The other was of a different type entirely, bedecked with lace and plumes, although his finery was somewhat stained from travel. He was handsome in a bold way, and his restless eyes shifted from side to side, never still an instant.

The host brought wine and food to the rough-hewn table and then stood back in the shadows, like a somber image. His features, now receding into vagueness, now luridly etched in the firelight as it leaped and flickered, were masked in a beard which seemed almost animal-like in thickness. A great nose curved above this beard and two small red eyes stared unblinkingly at his guests.

"Who are you?" suddenly asked the younger man.

"I am the host of the Cleft Skull Tavern," sullenly replied the other. His tone seemed to challenge his questioner to ask further.

"Do you have many guests?" l'Armon pursued.

"Few come twice," the host grunted.

Kane started and glanced up straight into those small red eyes, as if he sought for some hidden meaning in the host's words. The flaming eyes seemed to dilate, then dropped sullenly before the Englishman's cold stare.

"I'm for bed," said Kane abruptly, bringing his meal to a close. "I must take up my journey by daylight."

"And I," added the Frenchman. "Host, show us to our chambers."

Black shadows wavered on the walls as the two followed their silent host down a long, dark hall. The stocky, broad body of their guide seemed to grow and expand in the light of the small candle which he carried, throwing a long, grim shadow behind him.

At a certain door he halted, indicating that they were to sleep there. They entered; the host lit a candle with the one he carried, then lurched back the way he had come.

In the chamber the two men glanced at each other. The only furnishings of the room were a couple of bunks, a chair or two and a heavy table.

"Let us see if there be any way to make fast the door," said Kane. "I like not the looks of mine host."

"There are racks on door and jamb for a bar," said Gaston, "but no bar."

"We might break up the table and use its pieces for a bar," mused Kane.

"Mon Dieu," said l'Armon, "you are timorous, m'sieu."

Kane scowled. "I like not being murdered in my sleep," he answered gruffly.

"My faith!" the Frenchman laughed. "We are chance met—until I overtook you on the forest road an hour before sunset, we had never seen each other."

"I have seen you somewhere before," answered Kane, "though I can not now recall where. As for the other, I assume every man is an honest fellow until he shows me he is a rogue; moreover, I am a light sleeper and slumber with a pistol at hand."

The Frenchman laughed again.

"I was wondering how m'sieu could bring himself to sleep in the room with a stranger! Ha! Ha! All right, m'sieu Englishman, let us go forth and take a bar from one of the other rooms."

Taking the candle with them, they went into the corridor. Utter silence reigned and the small candle twinkled redly and evilly in the thick darkness.

"Mine host hath neither guests nor servants," muttered Solomon Kane. "A strange tavern! What is the name, now? These German words come not easily to me —the Cleft Skull? A bloody name, i'faith."

They tried the rooms next to theirs, but no bar rewarded their search. At last they came to the last room at the end of the corridor. They entered. It was furnished like the rest, except that the door was provided with a small barred opening, and fastened from the outside with a heavy bolt, which was secured at one end to the door-jamb. They raised the bolt and looked in.

"There should be an outer window, but there is not," muttered Kane. "Look!"

The floor was stained darkly. The walls and the one bunk were hacked in places, great splinters having been torn away.

"Men have died in here," said Kane, somberly. "Is yonder not a bar fixed in the wall?"

"Aye, but 'tis made fast," said the Frenchman, tugging at it. "The—"

A section of the wall swung back and Gaston gave a quick exclamation. A small, secret room was revealed, and the two men bent over the grisly thing that lay upon its floor.

"The skeleton of a man!" said Gaston. "And behold, how his bony leg is shackled to the floor! He was imprisoned here and died."

"Nay," said Kane, "the skull is cleft—methinks mine host had a grim reason for the name of his hellish tavern. This man, like us, was no doubt a wanderer who fell into the fiend's hands."

"Likely," said Gaston without interest; he was engaged in idly working the great iron ring from the skeleton's leg bones. Failing in this, he drew his sword and with an exhibition of remarkable strength cut the chain which joined the ring on the leg to a ring set deep in the log floor.

"Why should he shackle a skeleton to the floor?" mused the Frenchman. "Monbleu! 'Tis a waste of good chain. Now, m'sieu," he ironically addressed the white heap of bones, "I have freed you and you may go where you like!"

"Have done!" Kane's voice was deep. "No good will come of mocking the dead."

"The dead should defend themselves," laughed l'Armon. "Somehow, I will slay the man who kills me, though my corpse climb up forty fathoms of ocean to do it."

Kane turned toward the outer door, closing the door of the secret room behind him. He liked not this talk which smacked of demonry and witchcraft; and he was in haste to face the host with the charge of his guilt.

As he turned, with his back to the Frenchman, he felt the touch of cold steel against his neck and knew that a pistol muzzle was pressed close beneath the base of his brain.

"Move not, m'sieu!" The voice was low and silky. "Move not, or I will scatter your few brains over the room."

The Puritan, raging inwardly, stood with his hands in air while l'Armon slipped his pistols and sword from their sheaths.

"Now you can turn," said Gaston, stepping back.

Kane bent a grim eye on the dapper fellow, who stood bareheaded now, hat in one hand, the other hand leveling his long pistol.

"Gaston the Butcher!" said the Englishman somberly. "Fool that I was to trust a Frenchman! You range far, murderer! I remember you now, with that cursed great hat off—I saw you in Calais some years agone."

"Aye—and now you will see me never again. What was that?"

"Rats exploring yon skeleton," said Kane, watching the bandit like a hawk, waiting for a single slight wavering of that black gun muzzle. "The sound was of the rattle of bones."

"Like enough," returned the other. "Now, M'sieu Kane, I know you carry considerable money on your person. I had thought to wait until you slept and then slay you, but the opportunity presented itself and I took it. You trick easily."

"I had little thought that I should fear a man with whom I had broken bread," said Kane, a deep timbre of slow fury sounding in his voice.

The bandit laughed cynically. His eyes narrowed as he began to back slowly toward the outer door. Kane's sinews tensed involuntarily; he gathered himself like a giant wolf about to launch himself in a death leap, but Gaston's hand was like a rock and the pistol never trembled.

"We will have no death plunges after the shot," said Gaston. "Stand still, m'sieu; I have seen men killed by dying men, and I wish to have distance enough between us to preclude that possibility. My faith—I will shoot, you will roar and charge, but you will die before you reach me with your bare hands. And mine host will have another skeleton in his secret niche. That is, if I do not kill him myself. The fool knows me not nor I him, moreover—"

The Frenchman was in the doorway now, sighting along the barrel. The candle, which had been stuck in a niche on the wall, shed a weird and flickering light which did not extend past the doorway. And with the suddenness of death, from the darkness behind Gaston's back, a broad, vague form rose up and a gleaming blade swept down. The Frenchman went to his knees like a butchered ox, his brains spilling from his cleft skull. Above him towered the figure of the host, a wild and terrible spectacle, still holding the hanger with which he had slain the bandit.

"Ho! ho!" he roared. "Back!"

Kane had leaped forward as Gaston fell, but the host thrust into his very face a long pistol which he held in his left hand.

"Back!" he repeated in a tigerish roar, and Kane retreated from the menacing weapon and the insanity in the red eyes.

The Englishman stood silent, his flesh crawling as he sensed a deeper and more hideous threat than the Frenchman had offered. There was something inhuman about this man, who now swayed to and fro like some great forest beast while his mirthless laughter boomed out again.

"Gaston the Butcher!" he shouted, kicking the corpse at his feet. "Ho! ho! My fine brigand will hunt no more! I had heard of this fool who roamed the Black Forest—he wished gold and he found death! Now your gold shall be mine; and more than gold—vengeance!"

"I am no foe of yours," Kane spoke calmly.

"All men are my foes! Look—the marks on my wrists! See— the marks on my ankles! And deep in my back—the kiss of the knout! And deep in my brain, the wounds of the years of the cold, silent cells where I lay as punishment for a crime I never committed!" The voice broke in a hideous, grotesque sob.

Kane made no answer. This man was not the first he had seen whose brain had shattered amid the horrors of the terrible Continental prisons.

"But I escaped!" the scream rose triumphantly. "And here I make war on all men... What was that?"

Did Kane see a flash of fear in those hideous eyes?

"My sorcerer is rattling his bones!" whispered the host, then laughed wildly. "Dying, he swore his very bones would weave a net of death for me. I shackled his corpse to the floor, and now, deep in the night, I hear his bare skeleton clash and rattle as he seeks to be free, and I laugh, I laugh! Ho! ho! How he yearns to rise and stalk like old King Death along these dark corridors when I sleep, to slay me in my bed!"

Suddenly the insane eyes flared hideously: "You were in that secret room, you and this dead fool! Did he talk to you?"

Kane shuddered in spite of himself. Was it insanity or did he actually hear the faint rattle of bones, as if the skeleton had moved slightly? Kane shrugged his shoulders; rats will even tug at dusty bones.

The host was laughing again. He sidled around Kane, keeping the Englishman always covered, and with his free hand opened the door. All was darkness within, so that Kane could not even see the glimmer of the bones on the floor.

"All men are my foes!" mumbled the host, in the incoherent manner of the insane. "Why should I spare any man? Who lifted a hand to my aid when I lay for years in the vile dungeons of Karlsruhe—and for a deed never proven? Something happened to my brain, then. I became as a wolf—a brother to these of the Black Forest to which I fled when I escaped.

"They have feasted, my brothers, on all who lay in my tavern—all except this one who now clashes his bones, this magician from Russia. Lest he come stalking back through the black shadows when night is over the world, and slay me—for who may slay the dead?—I stripped his bones and shackled him. His sorcery was not powerful enough to save him from me, but all men know that a dead magician is more evil than a living one. Move not, Englishman! Your bones I shall leave in this secret room beside this one, to—"

The maniac was standing partly in the doorway of the secret room, now, his weapon still menacing Kane. Suddenly he seemed to topple backward, and vanished in the darkness; and at the same instant a vagrant gust of wind swept down the outer corridor and slammed the door shut behind him. The candle on the wall flickered and went out. Kane's groping hands, sweeping over the floor, found a pistol, and he straightened, facing the door where the maniac had vanished. He stood in the utter darkness, his blood freezing, while a hideous muffled screaming came from the secret room, intermingled with the dry, grisly rattle of fleshless bones. Then silence fell.

Kane found flint and steel and lighted the candle. Then, holding it in one hand and the pistol in the other, he opened the secret door.

"Great God!" he muttered as cold sweat formed on his body. "This thing is beyond all reason, yet with mine own eyes I see it! Two vows have here been kept, for Gaston the Butcher swore that even in death he would avenge his slaying, and his was the hand which set yon fleshless monster free. And he—"

The host of the Cleft Skull lay lifeless on the floor of the secret room, his bestial face set in lines of terrible fear; and deep in his broken neck were sunk the bare fingerbones of the sorcerer's skeleton.

The Moon of Skulls *(Robert E. Howard)*

I. — A MAN COMES SEEKING

A GREAT black shadow lay across the land, cleaving the red flame of the red sunset. To the man who toiled up the jungle trail it loomed like a symbol of death and horror, a menace brooding and terrible, like the shadow of a stealthy assassin flung upon some candle-lit wall.

Yet it was only the shadow of the great crag which reared up in front of him, the first outpost of the grim foothills which were his goal. He halted a moment at its foot, staring upward where it rose blackly limned against the dying sun. He could have sworn that he caught the hint of a movement at the top, as he stared, hand shielding his eyes, but the fading glare dazzled him and he could not be sure. Was it a man who darted to cover? A man, or— ?

He shrugged his shoulders and fell to examining the rough trail which led up and over the brow of the crag. At first glance it seemed that only a mountain goat could scale it, but closer investigation showed numbers of finger holds drilled into the solid rock. It would be a task to try his powers to the utmost but he had not come a thousand miles to turn back now.

He dropped the large pouch he wore at his shoulder, and laid down the clumsy musket, retaining only his long rapier, dagger, and one of his pistols; these he strapped behind him, and without a backward glance over the darkening trail he had come, he started the long ascent.

He was a tall man, long-armed and iron-muscled, yet again and again he was forced to halt in his upward climb and rest for a moment, clinging like an ant to the precipitous face of the cliff.

Night fell swiftly and the crag above him was a shadowy blur in which he was forced to feel with his fingers, blindly, for the holes which served him as a precarious ladder.

Below him, the night noises of the tropical jungle broke forth, yet it appeared to him that even these sounds were subdued and hushed, as though the great black hills looming above threw a spell of silence and fear even over the jungle creatures.

On up he struggled, and now to make his way harder, the cliff bulged outward near its summit, and the strain on nerve and muscle became heart-breaking. Time and again a hold slipped and he escaped falling by a hair's breadth. But every fibre in his lean hard body was perfectly co-ordinated, and his fingers were like steel talons with the grip of a vice. His progress grew slower and slower but on he went until at last he saw the cliffy brow splitting the stars a scant twenty feet above him.

And even as he looked, a vague bulk heaved into view, toppled on the edge and hurtled down toward him with a great rush of air about it. Flesh crawling, he flattened himself against the cliff's face and felt a heavy blow against his shoulder, only a glancing blow, but even so it nearly tore him from his hold, and as he fought desperately to right himself, he heard a reverberating crash among the rocks far below. Cold sweat beading his brow, he looked up. Who—or what—had shoved that boulder over the cliff edge? He was brave, as the bones on many a battlefield could testify, but the thought of dying like a sheep, helpless and with no chance of resistance, turned his blood cold.

Then a wave of fury supplanted his fear and he renewed his climb with reckless speed. The expected second boulder did not come, however, and no living thing met his sight as he clambered up over the edge and leaped erect, sword flashing from its scabbard.

He stood upon a sort of plateau which debouched into a very broken hilly country some half mile to the west. The crag he had just mounted jutted out from the rest of the heights like a sullen promontory, looming above the sea of waving foliage below, now dark and mysterious in the tropic night.

Silence ruled here in absolute sovereignty. No breeze stirred the sombre depths below, and no footfall rustled amid the stunted bushes which cloaked the plateau, yet that boulder which had almost hurled the climber to his death had not fallen by chance. What beings moved among these grim hills? The tropical darkness fell about the lone wanderer like a heavy veil through which the yellow stars blinked evilly. The steams of the rotting jungle vegetation floated up to him as tangible as a thick fog, and making a wry face he strode away from the cliff, heading boldly across the plateau, sword in one hand and pistol in the other.

There was an uncomfortable feeling of being watched in the very air. The silence remained unbroken save for the soft swishing that marked the stranger's cat-like tread through the tall upland grass, yet the man sensed that living things glided before and behind him and on each side. Whether man or beast trailed him he knew not, nor did he care over-much, for he was prepared to fight human or devil who barred his way. Occasionally he halted and glanced challengingly about him, but nothing met his eye except the shrubs which crouched like short dark ghosts about his trail, blended and blurred in the thick, hot darkness through which the very stars seemed to struggle, redly.

At last he came to the place where the plateau broke into the higher slopes and there he saw a clump of trees blocked out solidly in the lesser shadows. He approached warily, then halted as his gaze, growing somewhat accustomed to the darkness, made out a vague form among the sombre trunks which was not a part of them. He hesitated. The figure neither advanced nor fled. A dim form of silent menace, it lurked as if in wait. A brooding horror hung over that still cluster of trees.

The stranger advanced warily, blade extended, closer, straining his eyes for some hint of threatening motion. He decided that the figure was human but he was puzzled at its lack of movement. Then the reason became apparent—it was the corpse of a black man that stood among those trees, held erect by spears through his body, nailing him to the boles. One arm was extended in front of him, held in place along a great branch by a dagger through the wrist, the index finger straight as if the corpse pointed stiffly—back along the way the stranger had come. The meaning was obvious; that mute grim signpost could have but one significance—death lay beyond. The man who stood gazing upon that grisly warning rarely laughed, but now he allowed himself the luxury of a sardonic smile. A thousand miles of land and sea—ocean travel and jungle travel—and now they expected to turn him back with such mummery—whoever they were. He resisted the temptation to salute the corpse, as an action wanting in decorum, and pushed on boldly through the grove, half expecting an attack from the rear or an ambush. Nothing of the sort occurred, however, and emerging from the trees, he found himself at the foot of a rugged incline, the first of a series of slopes. He strode stolidly upward in the night, nor did he even pause to reflect how unusual his actions must have appeared to a sensible man. The average man would have camped at the foot of the crag and waited for morning before even attempting to scale the cliffs. But this was no ordinary man. Once his objective was in sight, he followed the straightest line to it, without a thought of obstacles, whether day or night. What was to be done, must be done. He had reached the outposts of the kingdom of fear at dusk, and invading its inmost recesses by night seemed to follow as a matter of course.

As he went up the boulder-strewn slopes the moon rose, lending its air of illusion, and in its light the broken hills ahead loomed up like the black spires of wizards' castles. He kept his eyes fixed on the dim trail he was following, for he knew not when another boulder might come hurtling down the inclines. He expected an attack of any sort and, naturally, it was the unexpected which really happened.

Suddenly from behind a great rock stepped a man, an ebony giant in the pale moonlight, a long spear blade gleaming silver in his hand, his headpiece of ostrich plumes floating above him like a white cloud. He lifted the spear in a ponderous salute, and spoke in the dialect of the river-tribes: "This is not the white man's land. Who is my white brother In his own kraal and why does he come into the Land of Skulls?"

"My name is Solomon Kane." the white man answered in the same language. "I seek the vampire queen of Negari."

"Few seek. Fewer find. None return," answered the other cryptically.

"Will you lead me to her?"

"You bear a long dagger in your right hand. There are no lions—here."

"A serpent dislodged a boulder. I thought to find snakes in the bushes."

The giant acknowledged this interchange of subtleties with a grim smile, and a brief silence fell.

"Your life," said the black man presently, "is in my hand."

Kane smiled thinly. "I carry the lives of many warriors in my hand."

The negro's gaze travelled uncertainly up and down the shimmery length of the Englishman's sword. Then he shrugged his mighty shoulders and let his spear point sink to the earth.

"You bear no gifts," said he; "but follow me and I will lead you to the Terrible One, the Mistress of Doom, The Red Woman, Nakari, who rules the land of Negari."

He stepped aside, and motioned Kane to precede him, but the Englishman, his mind on a spear-thrust in the back, shook his head.

"Who am I that I should walk in front of my brother? We be two chiefs—let us walk side by side." In his heart Kane smiled that he should be forced to use such unsavoury diplomacy with a savage warrior, but he showed no sign. The giant bowed with a certain barbaric majesty and together they went up the hill trail, unspeaking.

Kane was aware that men were stepping from hiding places and falling in behind them, and a surreptitious glance over his shoulder showed him some two score warriors trailing out behind them in two wedge-shaped lines. The moonlight glittered on sleek bodies, on waving headgears and long, cruel spear blades.

"My brothers are like leopards," said Kane courteously; "they lie in the low bushes and no eyes see them; they steal through the high grass and no man hears their coming."

The black chief acknowledged the compliment with a courtly inclination of his lion-like head, that set the plumes whispering.

"The mountain leopard is our brother, oh chieftain. Our feet are like drifting smoke but our arms are like iron. When they strike, blood drips red and men die."

Kane sensed an undercurrent of menace in the tone. There was no actual hint of threat on which he might base his suspicions, but the sinister minor note was there. He said no more for a space and the strange band moved silently upward in the moonlight like a cavalcade of spectres.

The trail grew steeper and more rocky, winding in and out among crags and gigantic boulders. Suddenly a great chasm opened before them, spanned by a natural bridge of rock, at the foot of which the leader halted.

Kane stared at the abyss curiously. It was some forty feet wide, and looking down, his gaze was swallowed by impenetrable blackness, hundreds of feet deep, he knew. On the other side rose crags dark and forbidding.

"Here," said the chief, "begin the true borders of Nakari's realm."

Kane was aware that the warriors were casually closing in on him. His fingers instinctively tightened about the hilt of the rapier which he had not sheathed. The air was suddenly super-charged with tension.

"Here, too," the warrior chief said, "they who bring no gifts to Nakari—die!"

The last word was a shriek, as if the thought had transformed the speaker into a maniac, and as he screamed it, the great arm went back and then forward with a ripple of mighty muscles, and the long spear leaped at Kane's breast.

Only a born fighter could have avoided that thrust. Kane's instinctive action saved his life—the great blade grazed his ribs as he swayed aside and returned the blow with a flashing thrust that killed a warrior who jostled between him and the chief at that instant.

Spears flashed in the moonlight and Kane, parrying one and bending under the thrust of another, sprang out upon the narrow bridge where only one could come at him at a time.

None cared to be first. They stood upon the brink and thrust at him, crowding forward when he retreated, giving back when he pressed them. Their spears were longer than his rapier, but he more than made up for the difference and the great odds by his scintillant skill and the cold ferocity of his attack.

They wavered back and forth and then suddenly a giant leaped from among his fellows and charged out upon the bridge like a wild buffalo, shoulders hunched, spear held, low eyes gleaming with a look not wholly sane. Kane leaped back before the onslaught, leaped back again, striving to avoid that stabbing spear and to find an opening for his point. He sprang to one side and found himself reeling on the edge of the bridge with eternity gaping beneath him. The warriors yelled in savage exultation as he swayed and fought for his balance, and the giant on the bridge roared and plunged at his rocking foe.

Kane parried with all his strength—a feat few swordsman could have accomplished, off balance as he was—saw the cruel spear blade flash by his cheek—felt himself falling backward into the abyss. A desperate effort, and he gripped the spear shaft, righted himself and ran the spearman through the body. The giant's great red cavern of a mouth spouted blood and with a dying effort he hurled himself blindly against his foe. Kane, with his heels over the bridge's edge, was unable to avoid him and they toppled over together, to disappear silently into the depths below.

So swiftly had it all happened that the warriors stood stunned. The giant's roar of triumph had scarcely died on his lips before the two were falling into the darkness. Now the rest of the natives came out on the bridge to peer down curiously, but no sound came up from the dark void.

II. — THE PEOPLE OF THE STALKING DEATH

AS Kane fell he followed his fighting instinct, twisting in midair so that when he struck, were it ten or a thousand feet below, he would land on top of the man who fell with him.

The end came suddenly—much more suddenly than the Englishman had thought for. He lay half stunned for an instant, then looking up, saw dimly the narrow bridge banding the sky above him, and the forms of the warriors, limned in the moonlight and grotesquely foreshortened as they leaned over the edge. He lay still, knowing that the beams of the moon did not pierce the deeps in which he was hidden, and that to those watchers he was invisible. Then when they vanished from view he began to review his present plight. His opponent was dead, and only for the fact that his corpse had cushioned the fall, Kane would have been dead likewise, for they had fallen a considerable distance. As it was, the Englishman was stiff and bruised.

He drew his sword from the native's body, thankful that it had not been broken, and began to grope about in the darkness. His hand encountered the edge of what seemed a cliff. He had thought that he was on the bottom of the chasm and that its impression of great depth had been a delusion, but now he decided that he had fallen on a ledge, part of the way down. He dropped a small stone over the side, and after what seemed a very long time he heard the faint sound of its striking far below.

Somewhat at a loss as to how to proceed, he drew flint and steel from his belt and struck them to some tinder, warily shielding the light with his hands. The faint illumination showed a large ledge jutting out from the side of the cliff, that is, the side next the hills, to which he had been attempting to cross. He had fallen close to the edge and it was only by the narrowest margin that he had escaped sliding off it, not knowing his position.

Crouching there, his eyes seeking to accustom themselves to the abysmal gloom, he made out what seemed to be a darker shadow in the shadows of the wall. On closer examination he found it to be an opening large enough to admit his body standing erect. A cavern, he assumed, and though its appearance was dark and forbidding in the extreme, he entered, groping his way when the tinder burned out.

Where it led to, he naturally had no idea, but any action was preferable to sitting still until the mountain vultures plucked his bones. For a long way the cave floor tilted upward—solid rock beneath his feet—and Kane made his way with some difficulty up the rather steep slant, slipping and sliding now and then. The cavern seemed a large one, for at no time after entering it could he touch the roof, nor could he, with a hand on one wall, reach the other.

At last the floor became level and Kane sensed that the cave was much larger there. The air seemed better, though the darkness was just as impenetrable. Suddenly he stopped dead in his tracks. From somewhere in front of him there came a strange indescribable rustling. Without warning something smote him in the face and slashed wildly. All about him sounded the eerie murmurings of many small wings and suddenly Kane smiled crookedly, amused, relieved and chagrined. Bats, of course. The cave was swarming with them. Still, it was a shaky experience, and as he went on and the wings whispered through the vast emptiness of the great cavern, Kane's mind found space to dally with a bizarre thought—had he wandered into Hell by some strange means, and were these in truth bats, or were they lost souls winging through everlasting night? Then, thought Solomon Kane, I will soon confront Satan himself—and even as he thought this, his nostrils were assailed by a horrid scent, fetid and repellent. The scent grew as he went slowly on, and Kane swore softly, though he was not a profane man. He sensed that the smell betokened some hidden threat, some unseen malevolence, inhuman and deathly, and his sombre mind sprang at supernatural conclusions. However, he felt perfect confidence in his ability to cope with any fiend or demon, armoured as he was in unshakable faith of creed and the knowledge of the rightness of his cause. What followed happened suddenly. He was groping his way along when in front of him two narrow yellow eyes leaped up in the darkness—eyes that were cold and expressionless, too hideously close-set for human eyes and too high for any four-legged beast. What horror had thus reared itself up in front of him?

This is Satan, thought Kane as the eyes swayed above him, and the next instant he was battling for his life with the darkness that seemed to have taken tangible form and thrown itself about his body and limbs in great slimy coils. Those coils lapped his sword arm and rendered it useless; with the other hand he groped for dagger or pistol, flesh crawling as his fingers slipped from slick scales, while the hissing of the monster filled the cavern with a cold paean of terror.

There in the black dark to the accompaniment of the bats' leathery rustlings, Kane fought like a rat in the grip of a mouse-snake, and he could feel his ribs giving and his breath going before his frantic left hand closed on his dagger hilt.

Then with a volcanic twist and wrench of his steel-thewed body he tore his left arm partly free and plunged the keen blade again and again to the hilt in the sinuous writhing terror which enveloped him, feeling at last the quivering coils loosen and slide from his limbs to lie about his feet like huge cables.

The mighty serpent lashed wildly in its death struggles, and Kane, avoiding its bone-shattering blows, reeled away in the darkness, labouring for breath, If his antagonist had not been Satan himself, it had been Satan's nearest earthly satellite, thought Solomon, hoping devoutly that he would not be called upon to battle another in the darkness there.

It seemed to him that he had been walking through the blackness for ages, and he began to wonder if there were any end to the cave, when a glimmer of light pierced the darkness. He thought it to be an outer entrance a great way off, and started forward swiftly, but to his astonishment, he brought up short against a blank wall after taking a few strides.

Then he perceived that the light came through a narrow crack in the wall, and feeling over this wall he found it to be of different material from the rest of the cave, consisting, apparently, of regular blocks of stone joined together with mortar of some sort—an indubitably man-built wall. The light streamed between two of these stones where the mortar had crumbled away. Kane ran his hands over the surface with an interest beyond his present needs. The work seemed very old and very much superior to what might be expected of a tribe of ignorant savages. He felt the thrill of the explorer and discoverer. Certainly no white man had ever seen this place and lived to tell of it, for when he had landed on the dank West Coast some months before, preparing to plunge into the interior, he had had no hint of such a country as this. The few white men who knew anything at all of Africa with whom he had talked, had never even mentioned the Land of Skulls, or the she-fiend who ruled it.

Kane thrust against the wall cautiously. The structure seemed weakened from age—a vigorous shove and it gave perceptibly. He hurled himself against it with all his weight—and a whole section of wall gave way with a crash, precipitating him into a dimly lighted corridor amid a heap of stone, dust and mortar.

He sprang up and looked about, expecting the noise to bring a horde of wild spearmen. Utter silence reigned. The corridor in which he now stood was much like a long narrow cave itself, save that it was the work of man. It was several feet wide and the roof was many feet above his head. Dust lay ankle-deep on the floor as if no foot had trod there for countless centuries, and the dim light, Kane decided, filtered in somehow through the roof or ceiling, for nowhere did he see any doors or windows. At last he decided the source was the ceiling itself, which was of a peculiar phosphorescent quality.

He set off down the corridor, feeling uncomfortably like a grey ghost moving along the grey halls of death and decay. The evident antiquity of his surroundings depressed him, making him sense vaguely the fleeting and futile existence of mankind. That he was now on top of the earth he believed, since light of a sort came in, but where, he could not even offer a conjecture. This was a land of enchantment—a land of horror and fearful mysteries, the jungle and river natives had said, and he had gotten whispered hints of its terrors ever since he had set his back to the Slave Coast and ventured into the hinterlands alone. Now and then he caught a low indistinct murmur which seemed to come through one of the walls, and he at last came to the conclusion that he had stumbled onto a secret passage in some castle or house. The natives who had dared speak to him of Negari, had whispered of a ju-ju city built of stone, set high amid the grim black crags of the fetish hills.

Then, thought Kane, it may be that I have blundered upon the very thing I sought and am in the midst of that city of terror. He halted, and choosing a place at random, began to loosen the mortar with his dagger. As he worked he again heard that low murmur, increasing in volume as he bored through the wall, and presently the point pierced through, and looking through the aperture it had made, he saw a strange and fantastic scene.

He was looking into a great chamber, whose walls and floors were of stone, and whose mighty roof was upheld by gigantic stone columns, strangely carved. Ranks of feathered black warriors lined the walls and a double column of them stood like statues before a throne set between two stone dragons which were larger than elephants. These men he recognized, by their bearing and general appearance, to be tribesmen of the warriors he had fought at the chasm. But his gaze was drawn irresistibly to the great, grotesquely ornamented throne. There, dwarfed by the ponderous splendour about her, a woman reclined. A tawny woman she was, young and of a tigerish comeliness. She was naked except for a be plumed helmet, armbands, anklets and a girdle of coloured ostrich feathers, and she sprawled upon the silken cushions with her limbs thrown about in voluptuous abandon. Even at that distance Kane could make out that her features were regal yet barbaric, haughty and Imperious, yet sensual, and with a touch of ruthless cruelty about the curl of full red lips. Kane felt his pulse quicken. This could be no other than she whose crimes had become almost mythical—Nakari of Negari, demon queen of a demon city, whose monstrous lust for blood had set half a continent shivering. At least she seemed human enough; the tales of the fearful river tribes had lent her a supernatural aspect. Kane had half expected to see a loathsome semi-human monster out of some past and demoniacal age.

The Englishman gazed, fascinated though repelled. Not even in the courts of Europe had he seen such grandeur. The chamber and all its accoutrements, from the carven serpents twined about the bases of the pillars to the dimly seen dragons on the shadowy ceiling, were fashioned on a gigantic scale. The splendour was awesome—elephantine—inhumanly oversized, and almost numbing to the mind which sought to measure and conceive the magnitude thereof. To Kane it seemed that these things must have been the work of gods rather than men, for this chamber alone would dwarf most of the castles he had known in Europe.

The fighting men who thronged that mighty room seemed grotesquely incongruous. They were not the architects of that ancient place. As Kane realized this, the sinister importance of Queen Nakari dwindled. Sprawled on that august throne in the midst of the terrific glory of another age, she seemed to assume her true proportions, a spoiled, petulant child engaged in a game of make-believe and using for her sport a toy discarded by her elders. And at the same time a thought entered Kane's mind—who were these elders? Still, the child could become deadly in her game, as the Englishman soon saw. A tall and massive warrior came through the ranks fronting the throne, and after prostrating himself four times before it, remained on his knees, evidently waiting permission to speak. The queen's air of lazy indifference fell from her, and she straightened with a quick lithe motion that reminded Kane of a leopardess springing erect. She spoke, and the words came faintly to him as he strained his faculties to hear. She spoke in a language very similar to that of the river tribes.

"Speak!"

"Great and Terrible One," said the kneeling warrior, and Kane recognized him as the chief who had first accosted him on the plateau—the chief of the guards on the cliffs, "let not the fire of your fury consume your slave." The young woman's eyes narrowed viciously.

"You know why you were summoned, son of a vulture?"

"Fire of Beauty, the stranger called Kane brought no gifts."

"No gifts?" she spat out the words. "What have I to do with gifts?" The chief hesitated, knowing now that there was some special importance in this stranger.

"Gazelle of Negari, he came climbing the crags in the night like an assassin, with a dagger as long as a man's arm in his hand. The boulder we hurled down missed him, and we met him upon the plateau and took him to the Bridge-Across-the-Sky, where, as is the custom, we thought to slay him; for it was your word that you were weary of men who came wooing you."

"Fool," she snarled. "Fool!"

"Your slave did not know, Queen of Beauty. The strange man fought like a mountain leopard. Two men he slew and fell with the last one into the chasm, and so he perished, Star of Negari."

"Aye," the queen's tone was venomous. "The first great man who ever came to Negari! One who might have—rise, fool!"

The man got to his feet.

"Mighty Lioness, might not this one have come seeking—"

The sentence was never completed. Even as he straightened, Nakari made a swift gesture with her hand. Two warriors plunged from the silent ranks and two spears crossed in the chief's body before he could turn. A gurgling scream burst from his lips, blood spurted high in the air and the corpse fell flatly at the foot of the great throne.

The ranks never wavered, but Kane caught the sidelong flash of strangely red eyes and the involuntary wetting of thick lips. Nakari had half risen as the spears flashed, and now she sank back, an expression of cruel satisfaction on her beautiful face and a strange brooding gleam in her scintillant eyes.

An indifferent wave of her hand and the corpse was dragged away by the heels, the dead arms trailing limply in the wide smear of blood left by the passage of the body. Kane could see other wide stains crossing the stone floor, some almost indistinct, others less dim. How many wild scenes of blood and cruel frenzy had the great stone throne-dragons looked upon with their carven eyes?

He did not doubt, now, the tales told him by the river tribes. These people were bred in rapine and horror. Their prowess had burst their brains. They lived, like some terrible beast, only to destroy. There were strange gleams behind their eyes which at times lit those eyes with up-leading flames and shadows of Hell. What had the river tribes said of these mountain people who had ravaged them for countless centuries?

"That they were henchmen of death, who stalked among them, and whom they worshipped." Still the thought hovered in Kane's mind as he watched—who built this place, and why were these people evidently in possession? Fighting men such as they were could not have reached the culture evidenced by these carvings. Yet the river tribes had spoken of no other men than those upon which he now looked. The Englishman tore himself away from the fascination of the barbaric scene with an effort. He had no time to waste; as long as they thought him dead, he had more chance of eluding possible guards and seeking what he had come to find. He turned and set off down the dim corridor. No plan of action offered itself to his mind and one direction was as good as another. The passage did not run straight; it turned and twisted, following the line of the walls, Kane supposed, and found time to wonder at the evident enormous thickness of those walls. He expected at any moment to meet some guard or slave, but as the corridors continued to stretch empty before him, with the dusty floors unmarked by any footprint, he decided that either the passages were unknown to the people of Negari or else for some reason were never used.

He kept a close lookout for secret doors, and at last found one, made fast on the inner side with a rusty bolt set in a groove of the wall. This he manipulated cautiously, and presently with a creaking which seemed terrifically loud in the stillness the door swung inward. Looking out he saw no one, and stepping warily through the opening, he drew the door to behind him, noting that it assumed the part of a fantastic picture painted on the wall. He scraped a mark with his dagger at the point where he believed the hidden spring to be on the outer side, for he knew not when he might need to use the passage again.

He was in a great hall, through which ran a maze of giant pillars much like those of the throne chamber. Among them he felt like a child in some great forest, yet they gave him some slight sense of security since he believed that, gliding among them like a ghost through a jungle, he could elude the warriors in spite of their craft.

He set off, choosing his direction at random and going carefully. Once he heard a mutter of voices, and leaping upon the base of a column, clung there while two women passed directly beneath him, but besides these he encountered no one. It was an uncanny sensation, passing through this vast hall which seemed empty of human life, but in some other part of which Kane knew there might be throngs of people, hidden from sight by the pillars.

At last, after what seemed an eternity of following these monstrous mazes, he came upon a huge wall which seemed to be either a side of the hall, or a partition, and continuing along this, he saw in front of him a doorway before which two spearmen stood like black statues.

Kane, peering about the corner of a column base, made out two windows high in the wall, one on each side of the door, and noting the ornate carvings which covered the walls, determined on a desperate plan.

He felt it imperative that he should see what lay within that room. The fact that it was guarded suggested that the room beyond the door was either a treasure chamber or a dungeon, and he felt sure that his ultimate goal would prove to be a dungeon.

Kane retreated to a point out of sight of the guards and began to scale the wall, using the deep carvings for hand and foot holds. It proved even easier than he had hoped, and having climbed to a point level with the windows, he crawled cautiously along a horizontal line, feeling like an ant on a wall. The guards far below him never looked up, and finally he reached the nearer window and drew himself up over the sill. He looked down into a large room, empty of life, but equipped in a manner sensuous and barbaric. Silken couches and velvet cushions dotted the floor in profusion, and tapestries heavy with gold work hung upon tile walls. The ceiling too was worked in gold.

Strangely incongruous, crude trinkets of ivory and ironwood, unmistakably savage in workmanship, littered the place, symbolic enough of this strange kingdom where signs of barbarism vied with a strange culture. The outer door was shut and in the wall opposite was another door, also closed.

Kane descended from the window, sliding down the edge of a tapestry as a sailor slides down a sail-rope, and crossed the room. His feet sank noiselessly into the deep fabric of the rug which covered the floor, and which, like all the other furnishings, seemed ancient to the point of decay.

At the door he hesitated. To step into the next room might be a desperately hazardous thing to do; should it prove to be filled with warriors, his escape was cut off by the spearmen outside the other door. Still, he was used to taking all sorts of wild chances, and now, sword in hand, he flung the door open with a suddenness intended to numb with surprise for an instant any foe who might be on the other side. Kane took a swift step within, ready for anything—then halted suddenly, struck speechless and motionless for a second. He had come thousands of miles in search of something, and there before him lay the object of his search.

III. — LILITH

A COUCH stood in the middle of the room, and on its silken surface lay a woman—a woman whose skin was fair and whose reddish gold hair fell about her bare shoulders. She now sprang erect, fright flooding her fine grey eyes, lips parted to utter a cry which she as suddenly checked.

"You!" she exclaimed. "How did you—?"

Solomon Kane closed the door behind him and came toward her, a rare smile on his dark face.

"You remember me, do you not, Marylin?"

The fear had already faded from her eyes even before he spoke, to be replaced by a look of incredible wonder and dazed bewilderment.

"Captain Kane! I can not understand—it seemed no one would ever come—"

She drew a small hand wearily across her brow, swaying suddenly.

Kane caught her in his arms—she was only a child—and laid her gently on the couch. There, chafing her wrists gently, he talked in a low hurried monotone, keeping an eye on the door all the time—which door, by the way, seemed to be the only entrance or egress from the room. While he talked he mechanically took in the chamber, noting that it was almost a duplicate of the outer room as regards hangings and general furnishings.

"First," said he, "before, we go into any other matters, tell me, are you closely guarded?"

"Very closely, sir," she murmured hopelessly, "I know not how you came here, but we can never escape."

"Let me tell you swiftly how I came to be here, and mayhap you will be more hopeful when I tell you of the difficulties already overcome. Lie still now, Marylin, and I will tell you how I came to seek an English heiress in the devil city of Negari.

"I killed Sir John Taferel in a duel. As to the reason, 'tis neither here nor there, but slander and a black lie lay behind it. Ere he died he confessed that he had committed a foul crime some years agone. You remember, of course, the affection cherished for you by your cousin, old Lord Hildred Taferal, Sir John's uncle? Sir John feared that the old lord, dying without issue, might leave the great Taferal estates to you.

"Years ago you disappeared, and Sir John spread the rumour that you had drowned. Yet when he lay dying with my rapier through his body, he gasped out that he had kidnapped you and sold you to a Barbary rover, whom he named—a bloody pirate whose name has not been unknown on England's coasts aforetime. So I came seeking you, and a long weary trail it has been, stretching into long leagues and bitter years.

"First I sailed the seas searching for El Gar, the Barbary corsair named by Sir John. I found him in the crash and roar of an ocean battle; he died, but even as he lay dying he told me that he had sold you in turn to a merchant out of Stamboul. So to the Levant I went and there by chance came upon a Greek sailor whom the Moors had crucified on the shore for piracy. I cut him down and asked him the question I asked all men—if he had in his wanderings seen a captive English girl-child with yellow curls. I learned that he had been one of the crew of the Stamboul merchants, and that she had, on her homeward voyage, been set upon by a Portuguese slaver and sunk—this renegade Greek and the child being among the few who were taken aboard the slaver.

"This slaver then, cruising south for black ivory, had been ambushed in a small bay on the African West Coast, and of your further fate the Greek knew nothing, for he had escaped the general massacre, and taking to sea in an open boat, had been taken up by a ship of Genoese freebooters.

"To the West Coast, then, I came, on the slim chance that you still lived, and there heard among the natives that some years ago a white child had been taken from a ship whose crew had been slain, and sent inland as a part of the tribute the shore tribes paid to the upper river chiefs.

"Then all traces ceased. For months I wandered without a clue as to your whereabouts, nay, without a hint that you even lived. Then I chanced to hear among the river tribes of the demon city Negari and the evil queen who kept a foreign woman for a slave. I came here."

Kane's matter-of-fact tone, his unfurbished narration, gave no hint of the full meaning of that tale—of what lay behind those calm and measured words—the sea-fights and the land fights— the years of privation and heart-breaking toil, the ceaseless danger, the everlasting wandering through hostile and unknown lands, the tedious and deadening labour of ferreting out the information he wished from ignorant, sullen and unfriendly savages.

"I came here," said Kane simply, but what a world of courage and effort was symbolized by that phrase! A long red trail, black shadows and crimson shadows weaving a devil's dance—marked by flashing swords and the smoke of battle—by faltering words falling like drops of blood from the lips of dying men.

Not a consciously dramatic man, certainly, was Solomon Kane. He told his tale in the same manner in which he had overcome terrific obstacles—coldly, briefly and without heroics.

"You see, Marylin," he concluded gently, "I have not come this far and done this much, to now meet with defeat. Take heart, child. We will find a way out of this fearful place."

"Sir John took me on his saddlebow." the girl said dazedly, and speaking slowly as if her native language came strangely to her from years of unuse, as she framed in halting words an English evening of long ago. "He carried me to the seashore where a galley's boat waited, filled with fierce men, dark and moustached and having scimitars, and great rings to the fingers. The captain, a Moslem with a face like a hawk, took me, a-weeping with fear, and bore me to his galley. Yet he was kind to me in his way, I being little more than a baby, and at last sold me to a Turkish merchant, as he told you. This merchant he met off the southern coast of France, after many days of sea travel.

"This man did not use me badly, yet I feared him, for he was a man of cruel countenance and made me understand that I was to be sold to a black sultan of the Moors. However, in the Gates of Hercules his ship was set upon by a Cadiz slaver and things came about as you have said.

"The captain of the slaver believed me to be the child of some wealthy English family and intended holding me for ransom, but in a grim darksome bay on the African coast he perished with all his men except the Greek you have mentioned, and I was taken captive by a savage chieftain.

"I was terribly afraid and thought he would slay me, but he did me no harm and sent me upcountry with an escort, who also bore much loot taken from the ship. This loot, together with myself, was, as you know, intended for a powerful king of the river peoples. But it never reached him, for a roving band of Negari fell upon the beach warriors and slew them all. Then I was taken to this city, and have since remained, slave to Queen Nakari.

"How I have lived through all those terrible scenes of battle and cruelty and murder, I know not.'

"A providence has watched over you, child," said Kane, "the power which doth care for weak women and helpless children, which led me to you in spite of all hindrances, and which shall yet lead us forth from this place, God willing."

"My people!" she exclaimed suddenly like one awaking from a dream, "what of them?"

"All in good health and fortune, child, save that they have sorrowed for you through the long years. Nay, old Sir Mildred hath the gout and doth so swear thereat that I fear for his soul at times. Yet methinks that the sight of you, little Marylin, would mend him."

"Still, Captain Kane," said the girl, "I can not understand why you came alone."

"Your brothers would have come with me, child, but it was not sure that you lived, and I was loth that any other Taferal should die in a land far from good English soil. I rid the country of an evil Taferal—'twas but just I should restore in his place a good Taferal, if so be she still lived—I, and I alone."

This explanation Kane himself believed. He never sought to analyse his motives and he never wavered once his mind was made up. Though he always acted on impulse, he firmly believed that all his actions were governed by cold and logical reasonings. He was a man born out of his time—a strange blending of Puritan and Cavalier, with a touch of the ancient philosopher, and more than a touch of the pagan, though the last assertion would have shocked him unspeakably. An atavist of the days of blind chivalry he was, a knight errant in the sombre domes of a fanatic. A hunger in his soul drove him on and on, an urge to right all wrongs, protect all weaker things, avenge all crimes against right and justice. Wayward and restless as the wind, he was consistent in only one respect—he was true to his ideals of justice and right. Such was Solomon Kane.

"Marylin," he now said kindly, taking her small hands in his sword-calloused fingers, "methinks you have changed greatly in the years. You were a rosy and chubby little maid when I used to dandle you on my knee in old England. Now you seem drawn and pale of face, though you are beautiful as the nymphs of the heathen books. There are haunting ghosts in your eyes, child—do they misuse you here?"

She lay back on the couch and the blood drained slowly from her already pallid features until she was deathly white. Kane bent over her, startled. Her voice came in a whisper.

"Ask me not. There are deeds better hidden in the darkness of night and forgetfulness. There are sights which blast the eyes and leave their burning mark forever on the brain. The walls of ancient cities, recked not of by men, have looked upon scenes not to be spoken of, even in whispers."

Her eyes closed wearily and Kane's troubled, sombre eyes unconsciously traced the thin blue lines of her veins, prominent against the unnatural whiteness of her skin.

"Here Is some demoniacal thing," he muttered. "A mystery—"

"Aye," murmured the girl, "a mystery that was old when Egypt was young! And nameless evil more ancient than dark Babylon— that spawned in terrible black cities when the world was young and strange."

Kane frowned, troubled. At the girl's strange words he felt an eery crawling fear at the back of his brain, as if dim racial memories stirred in the eon-deep gulfs, conjuring up grim chaotic visions, illusive and nightmarish.

Suddenly Marylin sat erect, her eyes flaring wide with fright. Kane heard a door open somewhere.

"Nakari!" whispered the girl urgently.

"Swift! She must not find you here! Hide quickly, and—" as Kane turned "—keep silent, whatever may chance!"

She lay back on the couch, feigning slumber as Kane crossed the room and concealed himself behind some tapestries which, hanging upon the wall, hid a niche that might have once held a statue of some sort.

He had scarcely done so when the single door of the room opened and a strange barbaric figure stood framed in it. Nakari, queen of Negari, had come to her slave.

The woman was clad as she had been when he had seen her on the throne, and the coloured armlets and anklets clanked as she closed the door behind her and came into the room. She moved with the easy sinuousness of a she-leopard and in spite of himself the watcher was struck with admiration for her lithe beauty. Yet at the same time a shudder of repulsion shook him, for her eyes gleamed with vibrant and magnetic evil, older than the world.

"Lilith!" thought Kane. "She is beautiful and terrible as Purgatory. She is Lilith—that foul, lovely woman of ancient legend."

Nakari halted by the couch, stood looking down upon her captive for a moment, then with an enigmatic smile, bent and shook her. Marylin opened her eyes, sat up, then slipped from her couch and knelt before her savage mistress—an act which caused Kane to curse beneath his breath. The queen laughed and, seating herself upon the couch, motioned the girl to rise, and then put an arm about her waist and drew her upon her lap. Kane watched, puzzled, while Nakari caressed the girl in a lazy, amused manner. This might be affection, but to Kane it seemed more like a sated leopard teasing its victim. There was an air of mockery and studied cruelty about the whole affair.

"You are very soft and pretty, Mara," Nakari murmured lazily, "much prettier than the other girls who serve me. The time approaches, little one, for your nuptial. And a fairer bride has never been borne up the Black Stairs."

Marylin began to tremble and Kane thought she was going to faint. Nakari's eyes gleamed strangely beneath her long-lashed drooping lids, and her full red lips curved in a faint tantalizing smile. Her every action seemed fraught with some sinister meaning. Kane began to sweat profusely.

"Mara," said the queen, "you are honoured above all other girls, and yet you are not content. Think how the girls of Negari will envy you, Mara, when the priests sing the nuptial song and the Moon of Skulls looks over the black crest of the Tower of Death. Think, little bride of the Master, how many girls have given their lives to be his bride!"

And Nakari laughed in her hateful, musical way as at a rare jest. And then suddenly she stopped short. Her eyes narrowed to slits as they swept the room, and her whole body tensed. Her hand went to her girdle and came away with a long thin dagger. Kane sighted along the barrel of his pistol, finger against the trigger. Only a natural hesitancy against shooting a woman kept him from sending death into the savage heart of Nakari, for he believed that she was about to murder the girl.

Then, with a lithe, cat-like motion, she thrust the girl from her knees and bounded back across the room, her eyes fixed with blazing intensity on the tapestry behind which Kane stood. Had those keen eyes discovered him? He quickly learned.

"Who is there?" she rapped out fiercely.

"Who hides behind those hangings? I do not see you nor hear you, but I know someone is there!" Kane remained silent. Nakari's wild beast instinct had betrayed him, and he was uncertain as to what course to follow. His next actions depended on the queen.

"Mara!" Nakari's voice slashed like a whip, "who is behind those hangings? Answer me! Shall I give you a taste of the whip again?" The girl seemed incapable of speech. She cowered where she had fallen, her beautiful eyes full of terror. Nakari, her blazing gaze never wavering, reached behind her with her free hand and gripped a cord hanging from the wall. She jerked viciously. Kane felt the tapestries whip back on either side of him, and he stood revealed. For a moment the strange tableau held—the gaunt adventurer in his blood-stained, tattered garments, the long pistol gripped in his right hand—across the room the savage queen in her barbaric finery, one arm still lifted to the cord, the other hand holding the dagger in front of her— the imprisoned girl cowering on the floor. Then Kane spoke: "Keep silent, Nakari, or you die!" The queen seemed numbed and struck speechless by the sudden apparition. Kane stepped from among the tapestries and slowly approached her.

"You!" she found her voice at last. "You must be he of whom the guardsmen spake! There are not two other white men in Negari! They said you fell to your death! How then—"

"Silence!" Kane's voice cut in harshly on her amazed babblings; he knew that the pistol meant nothing to her, but she sensed the threat of the long blade in his left hand. "Marylin," still unconsciously speaking in the river tribes' language, "take cords from the hangings and bind her—" He was about the middle of the chamber now. Nakari's face had lost much of its helpless bewilderment and into her blazing eyes stole a crafty gleam. She deliberately let her dagger fall as in token of surrender, then suddenly her hands shot high above her head and gripped another thick cord. Kane heard Marylin scream, but before he could pull the trigger or even think, the floor fell beneath his feet and he shot down into abysmal blackness. He did not fall far and he landed on his feet; but the force of the fall sent him to his knees and even as he went down, sensing a presence in the

darkness beside him, something crashed against his skull and he
dropped into a yet blacker abyss of unconsciousness.

IV. — DREAMS OF EMPIRE

SLOWLY Kane drifted back from the dim realms where the
unseen assailant's bludgeon had hurled him. Something
hindered the motion of his hands, and there was a metallic
clanking when he sought to raise them to his aching, throbbing
head. He lay in utter darkness, but he could not determine
whether this was absence of light, or whether he was still
blinded by the blow. He dazedly collected his scattered faculties
and realized that he was lying on a damp stone floor, shackled by
wrist and ankle with heavy iron chains which were rough and
rusty to the touch.

How long he lay there, he never knew. The silence was broken
only by the drumming pulse in his own aching head and the
scamper and chattering of rats. At last a red glow sprang up in
the darkness and grew before his eyes. Framed in the grisly
radiance rose the sinister and sardonic face of Nakari. Kane
shook his head, striving to rid himself of the illusion. But the
light grew and as his eyes accustomed themselves to it, he saw
that it emanated from a torch borne in the hand of the queen.

In the illumination he now saw that he lay in a small dank cell
whose walls, ceiling and floor were of stone. The heavy chains
which held him captive were made fast to metal rings set deep in
the wall. There was but one door, which was apparently of
bronze.

Nakari set the torch in a niche near the door, and coming
forward, stood over her captive, gazing down at him in a manner
rather speculating than mocking.

"You are he who fought the men on the cliff." The remark was an
assertion rather than a question. "They said you fell into the
abyss—did they lie? Did you bribe them to lie? Or how did you

escape? Are you a magician and did you fly to the bottom of the chasm and then fly to my palace? Speak!"

Kane remained silent. Nakari cursed.

"Speak or I will have your eyes torn out! I will cut your fingers off and burn your feet!" She kicked him viciously, but Kane lay silent, his deep sombre eyes boring up into her face, until the feral gleam faded from her eyes to be replaced by an avid interest and wonder.

She seated herself on a stone bench, resting her elbows on her knees and her chin on her hands.

"I never saw a white man before," she said.

"Are all white men like you? Bah! That cannot be! Most men are fools, black or white. I know that white men are not gods as the river tribes say—they are only men. I, who know all the ancient mysteries, say they are only men.

"But white men have strange mysteries too, they tell me—the wanderers of the river tribes and Mara. They have war clubs that make a noise like thunder and kill afar off—that thing which you held in your right hand, was that one of those clubs?"

Kane permitted himself a grim smile.

"Nakari, if you know all mysteries, how can I tell you aught that you know not already?"

"How deep and cold and strange your eyes are!" the queen said as if he had not spoken.

"How strange your whole appearance is—and you have the bearing of a king! You do not fear me—I never met a man who neither loved nor feared me. You would never fear me, but you could learn to love me. Look at me, bold one—am I not beautiful?"

"You are beautiful," answered Kane.

Nakari smiled and then frowned. "The way you say that, it is no compliment. You hate me, do you not?"

"As a man hates a serpent," Kane replied bluntly.

Nakari's eyes blazed with almost insane fury. Her hands clenched until the long nails sank into the palms; then as quickly as her anger had arisen, it ebbed away.

"You have the heart of a king." she said calmly, "else you would fear me. Are you a king in your land?"

"I am only a landless wanderer."

"You might be a king here," Nakari said slowly.

Kane laughed grimly. "Do you offer me my life?"

"I offer you more than that!" Kane's eyes narrowed as the queen leaned toward him, vibrant with suppressed excitement.

"Kane, what is it that you want more than anything else in the world?"

"To take the white girl you call Mara, and go."

Nakari sank back with an impatient exclamation.

"You can not have her; she is the promised bride of the Master. Even I could not save her, even if I wished. Forget her. I will help you forget her. Listen, listen to the words of Nakari, queen of Negari! You say you are a landless man—I will make you a king! I will give you the world for a toy! No, no, keep silent until I have finished," she rushed on, her words tumbling over each other in her eagerness. Her eyes blazed, her whole body quivered with dynamic intensity. "I have talked to travellers, to captives and slaves, men from far countries. I know that this land of mountains and rivers and jungle is not all the world. There are far-off nations and cities, and kings and queens to be crushed and broken.

"Negari is fading, her might is crumbling, but a strong man beside her queen might build it up again—might restore all her vanishing glory. Listen, Kane! Sit by me on the throne of Negari! Send afar to your people for the thunder-clubs to arm my warriors! My nation is still lord of central Africa. Together we will band the conquered tribes—call back the days when the realm of ancient Negari spanned the land from sea to sea! We will subjugate all the tribes of the river, the plain and the sea-shore, and instead of slaying them all, we will make one mighty army of them! And then, when all Africa is under our heel, we will sweep forth upon the world like a hungry lion to rend and tear and destroy!"

Solomon's brain reeled. Perhaps it was the woman's fierce magnetic personality, the dynamic power she instilled in her fiery words, but at the moment her wild plan seemed not at all wild and impossible. Lurid and chaotic visions flamed through the Puritan's brain—Europe torn by civil and religious strife, divided against herself, betrayed by her rulers, tottering—aye, Europe was in desperate straits now, and might prove an easy victim for some strong savage race of conquerors. What man can say truthfully that in his heart there lurks not a yearning for power and conquest?

For a moment the Devil sorely tempted Solomon Kane. Then before his mind's eye rose the wistful, sad face of Marylin Taferal, and Solomon cursed.

"Out on ye, daughter of Satan! Avaunt! Am I a beast of the forest to lead your savage devils against mine own people? Nay, no beast ever did so. Begone! If you wish my friendship, set me free and let me go with the girl."

Nakari leaped like a tiger-cat to her feet, her eyes flaming now with passionate fury. A dagger gleamed in her hand and she raised it high above Kane's breast with a feline scream of hate. A moment she hovered like a shadow of death above him; then her arm sank and she laughed. "Freedom? She will find her freedom when the Moon of Skulls leers down on the black altar. As for you, you shall rot in this dungeon. You are a fool; Africa's greatest queen has offered you her love and the empire of the world—and you revile her! You love the slave girl, perhaps? Until the Moon of Skulls she is mine and I leave you to think about this: that she shall be punished as I have punished her before—hung up by her wrists, naked, and whipped until she swoons!"

Nakari laughed as Kane tore savagely at his shackles. She crossed to the door, opened it, then hesitated and turned back for another word.

"This is a foul place, bold one, and maybe you hate me the more for chaining you here. Maybe in Nakari's beautiful throne room, with wealth and luxury spread before you, you will look upon her with more favour. Very soon I shall send for you, but first I will leave you here awhile to reflect. Remember—love Nakari and the kingdom of the world is yours; hate her—this cell is your realm."

The bronze door clanged sullenly, but more hateful to the imprisoned Englishman was the venomous, silvery laugh of Nakari.

Time passed slowly in the darkness. After what seemed a long time the door opened again, this time to admit a huge warrior who brought food and a sort of thin wine. Kane ate and drank ravenously and afterward slept. The strain of the last few days had worn him greatly, mentally and physically, but when he awoke he felt fresh and strong.

Again the door opened and two great savage warriors entered. In the light of the torches they bore, Kane saw that they were giants, clad in loin-cloths and ostrich plume headgear, and bearing long spears in their hands.

"Nakari wishes you to come to her, white man," was all they said, as they took off his shackles. He arose, exultant in even brief freedom, his keen brain working fiercely for a way of escape.

Evidently the fame of his prowess had spread, for the two warriors showed great respect for him. They motioned him to precede them, and walked carefully behind him, the points of their spears boring into his back. Though they were two to one, and he was unarmed, they were taking no chances. The gazes they directed at him were full of awe and suspicion.

Down a long, dark corridor they went, his captors guiding him with light prods of their spears, up a narrow winding stair, down another passageway, up another stair, and then they emerged into the vast maze of gigantic pillars into which Kane had first come. As they started down this huge hall, Kane's eyes suddenly fell on a strange and fantastic picture painted on the wall ahead of him. His heart gave a sudden leap as he recognized it. It was some distance in front of him and he edged imperceptibly toward the wall until he and his guards were walking along very close to it. Now he was almost abreast of the picture and could even make out the mark his dagger had made upon it.

The warriors following Kane were amazed to hear him gasp suddenly like a man struck by a spear. He wavered in his stride and began clutching at the air for support.

They eyed each other doubtfully and prodded him, but he cried out like a dying man and slowly crumpled to the floor, where he lay in a strange, unnatural position, one leg doubled back under him and one arm half-supporting his lolling body.

The guards looked at him fearfully. To all appearances he was dying, but there was no wound upon him. They threatened him with their spears, but he paid no heed. Then they lowered their weapons uncertainly and one of them bent over him.

Then it happened. The instant the guard stooped forward, Kane came up like a steel spring released. His right fist following his motion curved up from the hip in a whistling half-circle and crashed against the warrior's jaw. Delivered with all the power of arm and shoulder, propelled by the upthrust of the powerful legs as Kane straightened, the blow was like that of a sling-shot. The guard slumped to the floor, unconscious before his knees gave way.

The other warrior plunged forward with a bellow, but even as his victim fell, Kane twisted aside, and his frantic hand found the secret spring in the painting and pressed.

All happened in the breath of a second. Quick as the warrior was, Kane was quicker, for he moved with the dynamic speed of a famished wolf. For an instant, the falling body of the senseless guard hindered the other warrior's thrust, and in that instant Kane felt the hidden door give way. From the corner of his eye he saw a long gleam of steel shooting for his heart. He twisted about and hurled himself against the door, vanishing through it even as the stabbing spear slit the skin on his shoulder.

To the dazed and bewildered warrior, standing there with weapon upraised for another thrust, it seemed as if his prisoner had simply vanished through a solid wall, for only a fantastic picture met his gaze and this did not give to his efforts.

V. — "FOR A THOUSAND YEARS—"

KANE slammed the hidden door shut behind him, jammed down the spring and for a moment leaned against it, every muscle tensed, expecting to hold it against the efforts of a horde of spearmen. But nothing of the sort materialized. He heard his guard fumbling outside for a time; then that sound, too, ceased. It seemed impossible that these people should have lived in this palace as long as they had without discovering the secret doors and passages, but it was a conclusion which forced itself upon Kane's mind. At last he decided that he was safe from pursuit for the time being, and turning, started down the long, narrow corridor with its eon-old dust and its dim grey light. He felt baffled and furious, though he was free from Nakari's shackles. He had no idea how long he had been in the palace; it seemed ages. It must be day now, for it was light in the outer halls, and he had seen no torches after they had left the subterranean dungeons. He wondered if Nakari had carried out her threat of vengeance on the helpless girl, and swore passionately. Free for the time being, yes; but unarmed and hunted through this infernal palace like a rat. How could he aid either himself or Marylin? But his confidence never faltered. He was in the right, and some way would present itself. Suddenly a narrow stairway branched off the main passageway, and up this he went, the light growing stronger and stronger until he stood in the full glare of the African sunlight. The stair terminated in a sort of small landing directly in front of which was a tiny window, heavily barred. Through this he saw the blue sky tinted gold with the blazing sunlight; the sight was like wine to him and he drew in deep breaths of fresh, untainted air, breathing deep as if to rid his lungs of the aura of dust and decayed grandeur through which he had been passing.

He was looking out over a weird and bizarre landscape. Far to the right and the left loomed up great black crags and beneath them there reared castles and towers of stone, of strange architecture—it was as if giants from some other planet had thrown them up in a wild and chaotic debauch of creation. These buildings were backed solidly against the cliffs, and Kane knew that Nakari's palace also must be built into the wall of the crag behind it. He seemed to be in the front of that palace in a sort of minaret built on the outer wall. But there was only one window in it and his view was limited.

Far below him through the winding and narrow streets of that strange city, swarms of people went to and fro, seeming like black ants to the watcher above. East, north and south, the cliffs formed a natural bulwark; only to the west was a built wall.

The sun was sinking west. Kane turned reluctantly from the barred window and went down the stairs again. Again he paced down the narrow grey corridor, aimlessly and planlessly, for what seemed miles and miles. He descended lower and lower into passages that lay below passages. The light grew dimmer, and a dank slime appeared on the walls. Then Kane halted, a faint sound from beyond the wall arresting him. What was that? A faint rattle—the rattle of chains.

Kane leaned close to the wall, and in the semi-darkness his hand encountered a rusty spring. He worked at it cautiously and presently felt the hidden door it betokened swing inward. He gazed out warily.

He was looking into a cell, the counterpart of the one in which he had been confined. A smouldering torch was thrust into a niche on the wall, and by its lurid and flickering light he made out a form on the floor, shackled wrist and ankle as he had been shackled.

A man; at first Kane thought him to be a native, but a second glance made him doubt. His skin was dark, but his features were finely chiselled, and he possessed a high, magnificent forehead, hard vibrant eyes, and straight dark hair.

The man spoke in an unfamiliar dialect, one which was strangely distinct and clear-cut in contrast to the guttural jargon of the natives with whom Kane was familiar. The Englishman spoke in English, and then in the language of the river tribes.

"You who come through the ancient door," said the other in the latter dialect, "who are you? You are no savage—at first I thought you one of the Old Race, but now I see you are not as they. Whence come you?"

"I am Solomon Kane," said the Puritan, "a prisoner in this devil-city. I come from far across the blue salt sea."

The man's eyes lighted at the word.

"The sea! The ancient and everlasting! The sea which I have never seen, but which cradled the glory of my ancestors! Tell me, stranger, have you, like they, sailed across the breast of the great blue monster, and have your eyes looked on the golden spires of Atlantis and the crimson walls of Mu?"

"Truly," answered Solomon uncertainly. "I have sailed the seas, even to Hindustan and Cathay, but of the countries you mention I know nothing."

"Nay," the other sighed. "I dream—I dream. Already the shadow of the great night falls across my brain and my words wander. Stranger, there have been times when these cold walls and floor have seemed to melt into green, surging deeps and my soul was filled with the deep booming of the everlasting sea. I who have never seen the sea!"

Kane shuddered involuntarily. Surely this man was insane. Suddenly the other shot out a withered, claw-like hand and gripped his arm, despite the hampering chain.

"You whose skin is so strangely fair! Have you seen Nakari, the she-fiend who rules this crumbling city?"

"I have seen her," said Kane grimly, "and now I flee like a hunted rat from her murderers."

"You hate her!" the other cried. "Ha, I know! You seek Mara, the white girl who is her slave?"

"Aye."

"Listen," the shackled one spoke with strange solemnity. "I am dying. Nakari's rack has done its work. I die and with me dies the shadow of the glory that was my nation's. For I am the last of my race. In all the world there is none like me. Hark now, to the voice of a dying race."

And Kane, leaning there in the flickering semi-darkness of the cell, heard the strangest tale to which man has ever listened, brought out of the mist of the dim dawn ages by the lips of delirium. Clear and distinct the words fell from the dying man and Kane alternately burned and froze as vista after gigantic vista of time and space swept up before him.

"Long aeons ago—ages, ages ago—the empire of my race rose proudly above the waves. So long ago was it that no man remembers an ancestor who remembered it. In a great land to the west our cities rose. Our golden spires split the stars; our purple-prowed galleys broke the waves around the world, looting the sunset for its treasure and the sunrise for its wealth.

"Our legions swept forth to the north and to the south, to the west and the east, and none could stand before them. Our cities banded the world; we sent our colonies to all lands to subdue all savages, men of all colours, and enslave them. They toiled for us in the mines and at the galley's oars. All over the world the people of Atlantis reigned supreme. We were a sea-people, and we delved the deeps of all the oceans. The mysteries were known to us, and the secret things of land and sea and sky. We read the stars and were wise. Sons of the sea, we exalted him above all others.

"We worshipped Valka and Hotah, Honen and Golgor. Many virgins, many strong youths, died on their altars and the smoke of the shrines blotted out the sun. Then the sea rose and shook himself. He thundered from his abyss and the thrones of the world fell before him! New lands rose from the deep and Atlantis and Mu were swallowed up by the gulf. The green sea roared through the fanes and the castles, and the sea-weed encrusted the golden spires and the topaz towers. The empire of Atlantis vanished and was forgotten, passing into the everlasting gulf of time and oblivion. Likewise the colony cities in barbaric lands, cut off from their mother kingdom, perished. The savage barbarians rose and burned and destroyed until in all the world only the colony city of Negari remained as a symbol of the lost empire.

"Here my ancestors ruled as kings, and the ancestors of Nakari— the she-cat—bent the knee of slavery to them. Years passed, stretching into centuries. The empire of Negari dwindled. Tribe after tribe rose and flung off the chains, pressing the lines back from the sea, until at last the sons of Atlantis gave way entirely and retreated into the city itself—the last stronghold of the race. Conquerors no longer, hemmed in by ferocious tribes, yet they held those tribes at bay for a thousand years. Negari was invincible from without; her walls held firm; but within evil influences were at work. The sons of Atlantis had brought their slaves into the city with them. The rulers were warriors, scholars, priests, artisans; they did no menial work. For that they depended upon the slaves. There were more of these slaves than there were masters. And they increased while the sons of Atlantis dwindled.

"They mixed with each other more and more as the race degenerated until at last only the priestcraft was free of the taint of savage blood. Rulers sat on the throne of Negari who possessed little of the blood of Atlantis, and these allowed more and more wild tribesmen to enter the city in the guise of servants, mercenaries and friends.

"Then came a day when these fierce slaves revolted and slew all who bore a trace of the blood of Atlantis, except the priests and their families. These they imprisoned as 'fetish people'. For a thousand years savages have ruled in Negari, their kings guided by the captive priests, who though prisoners, were yet the masters of kings." Kane listened enthralled. To his imaginative mind, the tale burned and lived with strange fire from cosmic time and space.

"After all the sons of Atlantis, save the priests, were dead, there rose a great king to the defiled throne of ancient Negari. He was a tiger and his warriors were like leopards. They called themselves Negari, ravishing even the name of their former masters, and none could stand before them. They swept the land from sea to sea, and the smoke of destruction put out the stars. The great river ran red and the new lords of Negari strode above the corpses of their tribal foes. Then the great king died and the empire crumbled, even as the Atlantean kingdom of Negari had crumbled.

"They were skilled in war. The dead sons of Atlantis, their former masters, had trained them well in the ways of battle, and against the wild tribesmen they were invincible. But only the ways of war had they learned, and the empire was torn with civil strife. Murder and intrigue stalked redhanded through the palaces and the streets, and the boundaries of the empire dwindled and dwindled. All the while, savage kings with red, frenzied brains sat on the throne, and behind the curtains, unseen but greatly feared, the Atlantean priests guided the nation, holding it together, keeping it from absolute destruction.

"Prisoners in the city were we, for there was nowhere else in the world to go. We moved like ghosts through the secret passages in the walls and under the earth, spying on intrigue and doing secret magic. We upheld the cause of the royal family—the descendants of that tiger-like king of long ago—against all plotting chiefs, and grim are the tales which these silent walls could tell.

"These savages are not like the other natives of the region. A latent insanity lurks in the brains of every one. They have tasted so deeply and so long of slaughter and victory that they are as human leopards, forever thirsting for blood. On their myriad wretched slaves they have sated all lusts and desires until they have become foul and terrible beasts, forever seeking some new sensation, forever quenching their fearful thirsts in blood.

"Like a lion have they lurked in these crags for a thousand years, to rush forth and ravage the jungle and river people, enslaving and destroying. They are still invincible from without, though their possessions have dwindled to the very walls of this city, and their former great conquests and invasions have dwindled to raids for slaves.

"But as they faded, so too faded their secret masters, the Atlantean priests. One by one they died, until only I remained. In the last century they too have mixed with their rulers and slaves, and now—oh, the shame upon me!—I, the last son of Atlantis, bear in my veins the taint of barbarian blood. They died; I remained, doing magic and guiding the savage kings, I the last priest of Negari. Then the she-fiend, Nakari, arose."

Kane leaned forward with quickened interest. New life surged into the tale as it touched upon his own time.

"Nakari!" the name was spat as a snake hisses; "slave and the daughter of a slave! Yet she prevailed when her hour came and all the royal family died.

"And me, the last son of Atlantis, me she prisoned and chained. She feared not the silent Atlantean priests, for she was the daughter of a Satellite—one of the lesser, native priests. They were men who did the menial work of the masters—performing the lesser sacrifices, divining from the livers of fowls and serpents and keeping the holy fires for ever burning. Much she knew of us and our ways, and evil ambition burned in her.

"As a child she danced in the March of the New Moon, and as a young girl she was one of the Starmaidens. Much of the lesser mysteries was known to her, and more she learned, spying upon the secret rites of the priests who enacted hidden rituals that were old when the earth was young.

"For the remnants of Atlantis secretly kept alive the old worships of Valka and Hotah, Honen and Golgor, long forgotten and not to be understood by these savage people whose ancestors died screaming on their altars. Alone of all the savage Negari, she feared us not. Nakari not only overthrew the king and set herself on the throne, but she dominated the priests—the Satellites and the few Atlantean masters who were left. All these last, save me, died beneath the daggers of her assassins or on her racks. She alone of all the myriad savage thousands who have lived and died between these walls guessed at the hidden passages and subterranean corridors, secrets which we of the priestcraft had guarded jealously from the people for a thousand years.

"Ha! Ha! Blind, savage fools! To pass an ageless age in this city, yet never to learn of the secrets thereof! Apes—fools! Not even the lesser priests know of the long grey corridors, lit by phosphorescent ceilings, through which in bygone ages strange forms have glided silently. For our ancestors built Negari as they built Atlantis on a mighty scale and with an unknown art. Not for men alone did we build, but for the gods who moved unseen among us. And deep the secrets these ancient walls hold!

"Torture could not wring these secrets from our lips, but shackled in her dungeons, we trod our hidden corridors no more.

For years the dust has gathered there, untouched by human foot, while we, and finally I alone, lay chained in these foul cells. And among the temples and the dark, mysterious shrines of old, move vile Satellites, elevated by Nakari to glories that were once mine—for I am the last Atlantean high priest.

"Their doom is ascertained, and red will be their ruin' Valka and Golgor, gods lost and forgotten, whose memory shall die with me, strike down their walls and humble them unto the dust! Break the altars of their blind pagan gods—"

Kane realized that the man was wandering in his mind. The keen brain had begun to crumble at last.

"Tell me," said he; "you mentioned the fair girl. Mara. What do you know of her?"

"She was brought to Negari years ago by raiders," the other answered, "only a few years after the rise of the savage queen, whose slave she is. Little of her I know, for shortly after her arrival, Nakari turned on me—and the years that lie between have been grim dark years, shot red with torture and agony. Here I have lain, hampered by my chains from escape which lay in that door through which you entered—and for the knowledge of which Nakari has torn me on racks and suspended me over slow fires."

Kane shuddered. "You know not if they have so misused the white girl? Her eyes are haunted and she has wasted away."

"She has danced with the Starmaidens at Nakari's command, and has looked on the bloody and terrible rites of the Black Temple. She has lived for years among a people with whom blood is cheaper than water, who delight in slaughter and foul torture, and such sights as she has looked upon would blast the eyes and wither the flesh of strong men. She has seen the victims of Nakura die amid horrid torments, and the sight is burned forever in the brain of the beholder. The rites of the Atlanteans the savages took whereby to honour their own crude gods, and though the essence of those rites is lost in the wasting years, yet even Nakari's minions perform them; they are not such as men can look on, unshaken."

Kane was thinking, "A fair day for the world when this Atlantis sank, for most certainly it bred a race of strange and unknown evil." Aloud he said, "Who is this Master of whom Nakari spake, and what meant she by calling Mara his bride?"

"Nakura—Nakura. The skull of evil, the symbol of Death that they worship. What know these savages of the gods of sea-girt Atlantis? What know they of the dread and unseen gods whom their masters worshipped with majestic and mysterious rites? They understand not of the unseen essence, the invisible deity that reigns in the air and the elements; they must worship a material object, endowed with human shape. Nakura was the last great wizard of Atlantean Negari. A renegade he was, who conspired against his own people and aided the revolt of the savages. In life they followed him and in death they deified him. High in the Tower of Death his fleshless skull is set, and on that skull hinge the brains of all the people of Negari.

"Nay, we of Atlantis worshipped Death, but we likewise worshipped Life. These people worship only Death and call themselves Sons of Death. And the skull of Nakura has been to them for a thousand years the symbol of their power, the evidence of their greatness."

"Do you mean," Kane broke in impatiently on these ramblings, "that they will sacrifice the girl to their god?"

"In the Moon of Skulls she will die on the Black Altar."

"What in God's name is this Moon of Skulls?" Kane cried passionately.

"The full moon. At the full of each moon, which we name the Moon of Skulls, a virgin dies on the Black Altar before the Tower of Death, where centuries ago, virgins died in honour of Golgor, the god of Atlantis. Now from the face of the tower that once housed the glory of Golgor, leers down the skull of the renegade wizard, and the people believe that his brain still lives therein to guide the star of the city. For look ye, stranger, when the full moon gleams over the rim of the tower and the chant of the priests falls silent, then from the skull of Nakura thunders a great voice, raised in an ancient Atlantean chant, and the people fall on their faces before it.

"But hark, there is a secret way, a stair leading up to a hidden niche behind the skull, and there a priest lurks and chants. In days gone by one of the sons of Atlantis had this office, and by all rights of men and gods it should be mine this day. For though we sons of Atlantis worshipped our ancient gods in secret, these savages would have none of them. To hold our power we were devotees to their foul gods and we sang and sacrificed to him whose memory we cursed.

"But Nakari discovered the secret, known before only to the Atlantean priests, and now one of her Satellites mounts the hidden stair and yammers forth the strange and terrible chant which is but meaningless gibberish to him, as to those who hear it. I, and only I, know its grim and fearful meaning."

Kane's brain whirled in his efforts to formulate some plan of action. For the first time during the whole search for the girl, he felt himself against a blank wall. The palace was a labyrinth, a maze in which he could decide no direction. The corridors seemed to run without plan or purpose, and how could he find Marylin, prisoned as she doubtless was in one of the myriad chambers or cells? Or had she already passed over the borderline of life, or succumbed to the brutal torture-lust of Nakari?

He scarcely heard the ravings and mutterings of the dying man.

"Stranger, do you indeed live or are you but one of the ghosts which have haunted me of late, stealing through the darkness of my cell? Nay, you are flesh and blood—but you are a savage, even as Nakari's race are savages. Aeons ago when your ancestors were defending their caves against the tiger and the mammoth, with crude spears of flint, the gold spires of my people split the stars. They are gone and forgotten, and the world is a waste of barbarians. Let me, too, pass as a dream that is forgotten in the mists of the ages."

Kane rose and paced the cell. His fingers closed like steel talons as on a sword hilt and a blind red wave of fury surged through his brain. Oh God! to get his foes before the keen blade that had been taken from him—to face the whole city, one man against them all—

Kane pressed his hands against his temples.

"The moon was nearly full when last I saw it. But I know not how long ago that was. I know not how long I have been in this accursed palace, or how long I lay in that dungeon where Nakari threw me. The time of full moon may be past, and—oh merciful God!—Marylin may be dead already."

"Tonight is the Moon of Skulls," muttered the other; "I heard one of my jailers speak of it."

Kane gripped the dying man's shoulder with unconscious force.

"If you hate Nakari or love mankind, in God's name tell me how to save the child."

"Love mankind?" the priest laughed insanely.

"What has a son of Atlantis and a priest of forgotten Golgor to do with love? What are mortals but food for the jaws of the gods? Softer girls than your Mara have died screaming beneath these hands and my heart was as iron to their cries. Yet hate—" the strange eyes flamed with fearful light "—for hate I will tell you what you wish to know!

"Go to the Tower of Death when the moon is risen. Slay the false priest who lurks behind the skull of Nakura, and then when the chanting of the worshippers below ceases, and the masked slayer beside the Black Altar raises the sacrificial dagger, speak in a loud voice that the people can understand, bidding them set free the victim and offer up instead, Nakari, queen of Negari!

"As for the rest, afterward you must rely on your own craft and prowess if you come free."

Kane shook him.

"Swift! Tell me how I am to reach this tower!"

"Go back through the door whence you came." The man was sinking fast, his words dropped to whispers. "Turn to the left and go a hundred paces. Mount the stair you come to, as high as it goes. In the corridor where it ceases go straight for another hundred paces, and when you come to what seems a blank wall, feel over it until you find a projecting spring. Press this and enter the door which will open. You will then be out of the palace and in the cliffs against which it is built, and in the only one of the secret corridors known to the people of Negari. Turn to your right and go straight down the passage for five hundred paces. There you will come to a stair, which leads up to the niche behind the skull. The Tower of Death is built into the cliff and projects above it. There are two stairs—"

Suddenly the voice trailed out. Kane leaned forward and shook the man, and the priest suddenly rose up with a great effort. His eyes blazed with a wild and unearthly light and he flung his shackled arms wide.

"The sea!" he cried in a great voice. "The golden spires of Atlantis and the sun on the deep blue waters! I come!"

And as Kane reached to lay him down again, he slumped back, dead.

VI. — THE SHATTERING OF THE SKULL

KANE wiped the cold sweat from his pale brow as he hurried down the shadowy passage. Outside this horrible palace it must be night. Even now the full moon—the grim Moon of Skulls— might be rising above the horizon. He paced off a hundred paces and came upon the stair the dying priest had mentioned. This he mounted, and coming into the corridor above, he measured off another hundred paces and brought up short against what appeared to be a doorless wall. It seemed an age before his frantic fingers found a piece of projecting metal. There was a creak of rusty hinges as the hidden door swung open and Kane looked into a passageway darker than the one in which he stood.

He entered, and when the door shut behind him he turned to his right and groped his way along for five hundred paces. There the corridor was lighter; light sifted in from without, and Kane discerned a stairway. Up this he went for several steps, then halted, baffled. At a sort of landing the stairway became two, one leading away to the left, the other to the right. Kane cursed. He felt that he could not afford to make a mistake—time was too precious—but how was he to know which would lead him to the niche where the priest hid?

The Atlantean had been about to tell him of these stairs when struck by the delirium which precedes death, and Kane wished fervently that he had lived only a few moments longer.

At any rate, he had no time to waste; right or wrong, he must chance it. He chose the right hand stair and ran swiftly up it. No time for caution now.

He felt instinctively that the time of sacrifice was close at hand. He came into another passage and discerned by the change in masonry that he was out of the cliffs again and in some building—presumably the Tower of Death. He expected any moment to come upon another stair, and suddenly his expectations were realized—but instead of up, it led down. From somewhere in front of him Kane heard a vague, rhythmic murmur and a cold hand gripped his heart. The chanting of the worshippers before—the Black Altar!

He raced forward recklessly, rounded a turn in the corridor, brought up short against a door and looked through a tiny aperture. His heart sank. He had chosen the wrong stair and had wandered into some other building adjoining the Tower of Death.

He looked upon a grim and terrible scene. In a wide open space before a great black tower whose spire rose above the crags behind it, two long lines of savage dancers swayed and writhed. Their voices rose in a strange meaningless chant, and they did not move from their tracks.

From their knees upward their bodies swayed in fantastic rhythmical motions, and in their hands torches tossed and whirled, shedding a lurid shifting red light over the scene. Behind them were ranged a vast concourse of people who stood silent.

The dancing torchlight gleamed on a sea of glittering eyes and eager faces, In front of the dancers rose the Tower of Death, gigantically tall, black and horrific. No door or window opened in its face, but high on the wall in a sort of ornamented frame there leered a grim symbol of death and decay. The skull of Nakura! A faint, eery glow surrounded it, lit somehow from within the tower, Kane knew, and wondered by what strange art the priests had kept the skull from decay and dissolution so long.

But it was neither the skull nor the tower which gripped the Puritan's horrified gaze and held it. Between the converging lines of yelling, swaying worshippers there rose a great black altar. On this altar lay a slim, white shape.

"Marylin!" the word burst from Kane's lips in a great sob.

For a moment he stood frozen, helpless, struck blind. No time now to retrace his steps and find the niche where the skull priest lurked.

Even now a faint glow was apparent behind the spire of the tower, etching that spire blackly against the sky. The moon had risen. The chant of the dancers soared up to a frenzy of sound, and from the silent watchers behind them began a sinister low rumble of drums. To Kane's dazed mind it seemed that he looked on some red debauch of a lower Hell.

What ghastly worship of past aeons did these perverted and degenerate rites symbolize? Kane knew that these people aped the rituals of their former masters in their crude way, and even in his despair he found time to shudder at the thought of what those original rites must have been.

Now a fearful shape rose up beside the altar where lay the silent girl. A tall figure, entirely naked save for a hideous painted mask on his face and a great head-dress of waving plumes. The drone of the chant sank low for an instant, then rose up again to wilder heights. Was it the vibrations of their song that made the floor quiver beneath Kane's feet?

Kane with shaking fingers began to unbar the door. Naught to do now but to rush out barehanded and die beside the girl he could not save. Then his gaze was blocked by a giant form which shouldered in front of the door. A huge man, a chief by his bearing and apparel, leaned idly against the wall as he watched the proceedings. Kane's heart gave a great leap. This was too good to be true! Thrust in the chief's girdle was the pistol that he himself had carried! He knew that his weapons must have been divided among his captors. This pistol meant nothing to the chief, but he must have been taken by its strange shape and was carrying it as savages will wear useless trinkets. Or perhaps he thought it a sort of war-club. At any rate, there it was. And again, floor and building seemed to tremble.

Kane pulled the door silently inward and crouched in the shadows behind his victim like a great brooding tiger.

His brain worked swiftly and formulated his plan of action. There was a dagger in the girdle beside the pistol; the chief's back was turned squarely to him and he must strike from the left to reach the heart and silence him quickly. All this passed through Solomon's brain in a flash as he crouched.

The chief was not aware of his foe's presence until Kane's lean right hand shot across his shoulder and clamped on his mouth, jerking him backward. At the same instant the Puritan's left hand tore the dagger from the girdle and with one desperate plunge sank the keen blade home.

The warrior crumpled without a sound and in an instant Kane's pistol was in its owner's hand. A second's investigation showed that it was still loaded and the flint still in place. No one had seen the swift murder. Those few who stood near the doorway were all facing the Black Altar, enwrapped in the drama, which was there unfolding. As Kane stepped across the corpse, the chanting of the dancers ceased abruptly. In the instant of silence which followed, Kane heard, above the pounding of his own pulse, the night wind rustle the death-like plumes of the masked horror beside the altar. A rim of the moon glowed above the spire. Then, from high up on the face of the Tower of Death, a deep voice boomed out in a strange chant. Mayhap the priest who spoke behind the skull knew not what his words meant, but Kane believed that he at least mimicked the very intonation of those long-dead Atlantean acolytes. Deep, mystic, resonant the voice sounded out, like the endless flowing of long tides on the broad white beaches.

The masked one beside the altar drew himself up to his great height and raised a long, glimmering blade. Kane recognized his own sword, even as he levelled his pistol and fired—not at the masked priest but full at the skull which gleamed in the face of the tower. For in one blinding flash of intuition he remembered the dying Atlantean's words: "Their brains hinge on the skull of Nakura!"

Simultaneously with the crack of the pistol came a shattering crash; the dry skull flew into a thousand pieces and vanished, and behind it the chant broke off short in a death shriek. The rapier fell from the hand of the masked priest and many of the dancers crumpled to the earth, the others halting short, spellbound. Through the deathly silence which reigned for an instant, Kane rushed toward the altar; then all Hell broke loose.

A babel of bestial screams rose to the shuddering stars. For centuries, only their faith in the dead Nakura had held together the blood-drenched brains of the savage Negari. Now their symbol had vanished, had been blasted into nothing before their eyes. It was to them as if the skies had split, the moon fallen and the world ended. All the red visions which lurked at the backs of their corroded brains leaped into fearful life, all the latent insanity which was their heritage rose to claim its own, and Kane looked upon a whole nation turned to bellowing maniacs.

Screaming and roaring they turned on each other, men and women, tearing with frenzied fingernails, stabbing with spears and with daggers, beating each other with the flaming torches, while over all rose the roar of frantic human beasts.

With clubbed pistol Kane battered his way through the surging, writhing ocean of flesh, to the foot of the altar stairs. Nails raked him, knives slashed at him, torches scorched his garments, but he paid no heed.

Then as he reached the altar, a terrible figure broke from the struggling mass and charged him. Nakari, queen of Negari, crazed as any of her subjects, rushed upon the Englishman with dagger bared and eyes horribly aflame.

"You shall not escape this time!" she was screaming, but before she reached him a great warrior, dripping blood and blind from a gash across his eyes, reeled across her path and lurched into her. She screamed like a wounded cat and struck her dagger into him, and then groping hands closed on her. The blind giant whirled her on high with one dying effort, and her last scream knifed the din of battle as Nakari, last queen of Negari, crashed against the stones of the altar and fell shattered and dead at Kane's feet. Kane sprang up the black steps, worn deep by the feet of myriad priests and victims, and as he came, the masked figure, who had stood like one turned to stone, came suddenly to life. He bent swiftly, caught up the sword he had dropped and thrust savagely at the charging Englishman. But the dynamic quickness of Solomon Kane was such as few men could match. A twist and sway of his steely body and he was inside the thrust, and as the blade slid harmlessly between arm and chest, he brought down the heavy pistol barrel among the waving plumes, crushing headdress, mask and skull with one blow. Then ere he turned to the fainting girl who lay bound on the altar, he flung aside the shattered pistol and snatched his stolen sword from the nerveless hand which still grasped it, feeling a fierce thrill of renewed confidence at the familiar feel of the hilt. Marylin lay white and silent, her death-like face turned blindly to the light of the moon which shone calmly down on the frenzied scene. At first Kane thought her to be dead, but his searching fingers detected a faint flutter of pulse. He cut her bonds and lifted her tenderly— only to drop her again and whirl as a hideous, blood-stained figure of insanity came leaping and gibbering up the steps. Full upon Kane's outthrust blade the creature ran, and toppled back into the red swirl below, clawing beast-like at its mortal wound. Then beneath Kane's feet the altar rocked; a sudden tremor hurled him to his knees and his horrified eyes beheld the Tower of Death sway to and fro. Some horror of Nature was taking place, and this fact pierced the crumbling brains of the fiends who fought and screamed below. A new element entered into their shrieking, and then the Tower of Death swayed far out with a terrible and awesome majesty—broke from the rocking crags and—gave way with a thunder of crashing worlds. Great stones and shards of masonry came raining down, bringing death and destruction to hundreds of screaming humans below. One of these stones crashed to pieces on the altar beside Kane, showering him with dust.

"Earthquake!" he gasped, and smitten by this new terror he caught up the senseless girl and plunged recklessly down the cracking steps, hacking and stabbing a way through the crimson whirlpools of bestial humanity that still tore and ravened. The rest was a red nightmare in which Kane's dazed brain refused to record all its horrors. It seemed that for screaming crimson centuries he reeled through narrow winding streets where bellowing, screeching demons battled and died, among titanic walls and black columns that rocked against the sky and crashed to ruin about him, while the earth heaved and trembled beneath his staggering feet and the thunder of crashing towers filled the world.

Gibbering fiends in human shape clutched and clawed at him, to fade before his flailing sword, and falling stones bruised and battered him. He crouched as he reeled along, covering the girl with his body as best he could, sheltering her alike from blind stone and blinder human.

At last, when it seemed mortal endurance had reached its limit, he saw the great black outer wall of the city loom before him, rent from earth to parapet and tottering for its fall. He dashed through a crevice, and gathering his efforts, made one last sprint. And scarce was he out of reach than the wall crashed, falling inward like a great black wave.

The night wind was in his face and behind him rose the clamour of the doomed city as Kane staggered down the hill path that trembled beneath his feet.

VII. — THE FAITH OF SOLOMON

DAWN lay like a cool white hand on the brow of Solomon Kane. The nightmares faded from his soul as he breathed deep of the morning wind which blew up from the jungle far below his feet— a wind laden with the musk of decaying vegetation. Yet it was like the breath of life to him, for the scents were those of the clean natural disintegration of outdoor things, not the loathsome aura of decadent antiquity that lurks in the walls of eon-old cities—Kane shuddered involuntarily.

He bent over the sleeping girl who lay at his feet, arranged as comfortably as possible with the few soft tree branches he had been able to find for her bed. Now she opened her eyes and stared about wildly for an instant; then as her gaze met the face of Solomon, lighted by one of his rare smiles, she gave a little sob of thankfulness and clung to him.

"Oh, Captain Kane! Have we in truth escaped from yon fearful city? Now it seems all like a dream—after you fell through the secret door in my chamber Nakari later went to your dungeon as she told me—and returned in vile humour. She said you were a fool, for she had offered you the kingdom of the world and you had but insulted her. She screamed and raved and cursed like one insane and swore that she would yet, alone, build a great empire of Negari.

"Then she turned on me and reviled me, saying that you held me—a slave—in more esteem than a queen and all her glory. And in spite of my pleas she took me across her knees and whipped me until I swooned.

"Afterward I lay half senseless for a long time, and was only dimly aware that men came to Nakari and said that you had escaped. They said you were a sorcerer, for you faded through a solid wall like a ghost. But Nakari killed the men who had brought you from the cell, and for hours she was like a wild beast.

"How long I lay thus I know not. In those terrible rooms and corridors where no natural sunlight ever entered, one lost all track of time. But from the time you were captured by Nakari and the time that I was placed on the altar, at least a day and a night and another day must have passed. It was only a few hours before the sacrifice that word came you had escaped.

"Nakari and her Star-maidens came to prepare me for the rite." At the bare memory of that fearful ordeal she whimpered and hid her face in her hands. "I must have been drugged. I only know that they clothed me in the white robe of the sacrifice and carried me into a great black chamber filled with horrid statues.

"There I lay for a space like one in a trance, while the women performed various strange and shameful rites according to their grim religion. Then I fell into a swoon, and when I emerged I was lying bound on the Black Altar—the torches were tossing and the devotees chanting—behind the Tower of Death the rising moon was beginning to glow—all this I knew faintly, as in a deep dream. And as in a dream I saw the glowing skull high on the tower—and the gaunt, naked priest holding a sword above my heart, then I knew no more. What happened?"

"At about that moment," Kane answered, "I emerged from a building wherein I had wandered by mistake, and blasted their hellish skull to atoms with a pistol ball. Whereupon, all these people, being cursed from birth by demons, and being likewise possessed of devils, fell to slaying one another; in the midst of the tumult an earthquake cometh to pass which shakes the walls down. Then I snatch you up, and running at random, come upon a rent in the outer wall and thereby escape, carrying you, who seem in a swoon.

"Once only you awoke, after I had crossed the Bridge-Across-the-Sky, as the people of Negari called it, which was crumbling beneath our feet by reason of the earthquake. After I had come to these cliffs, but dared not descend them in the darkness, the moon being nigh to setting by that time, you awoke and screamed and clung to me, whereupon I soothed you as best I might, and after a time you fell into a natural sleep."

"And now what?" asked the girl.

"England!" Kane's deep eyes lighted at the word. "I find it hard to remain in the land of my birth for more than a month at a time; yet though I am cursed with the wanderlust, 'tis a name which ever rouses a glow in my bosom. And how of you, child?"

"Oh, heaven!" she cried, clasping her small hands. "Home! Something of which to be dreamed—never attained, I fear. Oh, Captain Kane, how shall we gain through all the vast leagues of jungle which lie between this place and the coast?"

"Marylin," said Kane gently, stroking her curly hair, "methinks you lack somewhat in faith, both in Providence and in me. Nay, alone I am a weak creature, having no strength or might in me; yet in times past hath God made me a great vessel of wrath and a sword of deliverance. And, I trust, shall do so again.

"Look you, little Marylin: in the last few hours as it were, we have seen the passing of an evil race and the fall of a foul empire. Men died by thousands about us, and the earth rose beneath our feet, hurling down towers that broke the heavens; yea, death fell about us in a red rain, yet we escaped unscathed.

"Therein is—more than the hand of man! Nay, a Power—the mightiest Power! That which guided me across the world, straight to that demon city—which led me to your chamber— which aided me to escape again and led me to the one man in all the city who would give the information I must have, the strange, evil priest of an elder race who lay dying in a subterranean cell—and which guided me to the outer wall, as I ran blindly and at random—for should I have come under the cliffs which formed the rest of the wall, we had surely perished. That same Power brought us safely out of the dying city, and safe across the rocking bridge—which shattered and sundered down into the chasm just as my feet touched solid earth!

"Think you that having led me this far, and accomplished such wonders, the Power will strike us down now? Nay! Evil flourishes and rules in the cities of men and the waste places of the world, but anon the great giant that is God rises and smites for the righteous, and they lay faith in him.

"I say this: this cliff shall we descend in safety, and yon dank jungle traverse in safety, and it is as sure that in old Devon your people shall clasp you again to their bosom, as that you stand here." And now for the first time Marylin smiled, with the quick eagerness of a normal young girl, and Kane sighed in relief. Already the ghosts were fading from her haunted eyes, and Kane looked to the day when her horrible experiences should be as a dimming dream. One glance he flung behind him, where beyond the scowling hills the lost city of Negari lay shattered and silent, amid the ruins of her own walls and the fallen crags which had kept her invincible so long, but which had at last betrayed her to her doom.

A momentary pang smote him as he thought of the myriad of crushed, still forms lying amid those ruins; then the blasting memory of their evil crimes surged over him and his eyes hardened.

"And it shall come to pass, that he who fleeth from the noise of the fear shall fall into the pit; and he that cometh up out of the midst of the pit shall be taken in the snare; for the windows from on high are open, and the foundations of the earth do shake.

"For Thou hast made of a city an heap; of a defended city a ruin; a palace of strangers to be no city; it shall never be built.

"Moreover, the multitude of Thy stranger shall be like small dust and the multitude of the terrible ones shall be as chaff that passeth suddenly away; yea, it shall be at an instant suddenly.

"Stay yourselves and wonder; cry ye out and cry; they are drunken but not with wine; they stagger but not with strong drink.

"Verily, Marylin," said Kane with a sigh, "with mine own eyes have I seen the prophecies of Isaiah come to pass. They were drunken but not with wine. Nay, blood was their drink and in that red flood they dipped deep and terribly."

Then taking the girl by the hand he started toward the edge of the cliff. At this very point had he ascended in the night—how long ago it seemed.

Kane's clothing hung in tatters about him. He was torn, scratched and bruised. But in his eyes shone the clear calm light of serenity as the sun came up, flooding cliffs and jungle with a golden light that was like a promise of joy and happiness.

The Hills of the Dead *(Robert E. Howard)*

I. — VOODOO

The twigs which N'Longa flung on the fire broke and crackled. The upleaping flames lighted the countenances of the two men. N'Longa, voodoo man of the Slave Coast, was very old. His wizened and gnarled frame was stooped and brittle, his face creased by hundreds of wrinkles. The red firelight glinted on the human finger-bones which composed his necklace.

The other was an Englishman, and his name was Solomon Kane. He was tall and broad-shouldered, clad in black close garments, the garb of the Puritan. His featherless slouch hat was drawn low over his heavy brows, shadowing his darkly pallid face. His cold deep eyes brooded in the firelight.

"You come again, brother," droned the fetish-man, speaking in the jargon which passed for a common language of black man and white on the West Coast. "Many moons burn and die since we make blood-palaver. You go to the setting sun, but you come back!"

"Aye," Kane's voice was deep and almost ghostly. "Yours is a grim land, N'Longa, a red land barred with the black darkness of horror and the bloody shadows of death. Yet I have returned."

N'Longa stirred the fire, saying nothing, and after a pause Kane continued.

"Yonder in the unknown vastness"—his long finger stabbed at the black silent jungle which brooded beyond the firelight— "yonder lie mystery and adventure and nameless terror. Once I dared the jungle—once she nearly claimed my bones. Something entered into my blood, something stole into my soul like a whisper of unnamed sin. The jungle! Dark and brooding —over leagues of the blue salt sea she has drawn me and with the dawn I go to seek the heart of her. Mayhap I shall find curious adventure—mayhap my doom awaits me. But better death than the ceaseless and everlasting urge, the fire that has burned my veins with bitter longing."

"She call," muttered N'Longa. "At night she coil like serpent about my hut and whisper strange things to me. Ai ya! The jungle call. We be blood brothers, you and I. Me, N'Longa, mighty worker of nameless magic! You go to the jungle as all men go who hear her call. Maybe you live, more like you die. You believe in my fetish work?"

"I understand it not," said Kane grimly, "but I have seen you send your soul forth from your body to animate a lifeless corpse."

"Aye! Me N'Longa! priest of the Black God! Now watch, I make magic."

Kane gazed at the old voodoo man who bent over the fire, making even motions with his hands and mumbling incantations. Kane watched, and he seemed to grow sleepy. A mist wavered in front of him, through which he saw dimly the form of N'Longa, etched dark against the flames. Then it faded out.

Kane awoke with a start, hand shooting to the pistol in his belt. N'Longa grinned at him across the flame, and there was a scent of early dawn in the air. The fetish-man held a long stave of curious black wood in his hands. This stave was carved in a strange manner, and one end tapered to a sharp point.

"This voodoo staff," said N'Longa, putting it in the Englishman's hand. "Where your guns and long knife fail, this save you. When you want me, lay this on your breast, fold your hands on it and sleep. I come to you in your dreams."

Kane weighed the thing in his hand, highly suspicious of witchcraft. It was not heavy, but seemed as hard as iron. A good weapon at least, he decided. Dawn was just beginning to steal over the jungle and the river.

II. — RED EYES

SOLOMON KANE shifted his musket from his shoulder and let the stock fall to the earth. Silence lay about him like a fog. Kane's lined face and tattered garments showed the effect of long bush travel. He looked about him.

Some distance behind him loomed the green, rank jungle, thinning out to low shrubs, stunted trees and tall grass. Some distance in front of him rose the first of a chain of bare, sombre hills, littered with boulders, shimmering in the merciless heat of the sun. Between the hills and the jungle lay a broad expanse of rough, uneven grasslands, dotted here and there by clumps of thorn trees.

An utter silence hung over the country. The only sign of life was a few vultures flapping heavily across the distant hills. For the last few days Kane had noticed the increasing number of these unsavoury birds. The sun was rocking westward but its heat was in no way abated.

Trailing his musket he started forward slowly. He had no objective in view. This was all unknown country and one direction was as good as another. Many weeks ago he had plunged into the jungle with the assurance born of courage and ignorance. Having by some miracle survived the first few weeks, he was becoming hard and toughened, able to hold his own with any of the grim denizens of the fastness he dared.

As he progressed he noted an occasional lion spoor but there seemed to be no animals in the grasslands—none that left tracks, at any rate. Vultures sat like black, brooding images in some of the stunted trees, and suddenly he saw an activity among them some distance beyond. Several of the dusky birds circled about a clump of high grass, dipping, then rising again. Some beast of prey was defending his kill against them, Kane decided, and wondered at the lack of snarling and roaring which usually accompanied such scenes. His curiosity was roused and he turned his steps in that direction.

At last, pushing through the grass which rose about his shoulders, he saw, as through a corridor walled with the rank waving blades, a ghastly sight. The corpse of a black man lay, face down, and as the Englishman looked, a great dark snake rose and slid away into the grass, moving so quickly that Kane was unable to decide its nature. But it had a weird human-like suggestion about it.

Kane stood over the body, noting that while the limbs lay awry as if broken, the flesh was not torn as a lion or leopard would have torn it. He glanced up at the whirling vultures and was amazed to see several of them skimming along close to the earth, following a waving of the grass which marked the flight of the thing which had presumably slain the black man. Kane wondered what thing the carrion birds, which eat only the dead, were hunting through the grasslands. But Africa is full of never-explained mysteries.

Kane shrugged his shoulders and lifted his musket again. Adventures he had had in plenty since he parted from N'Longa some moons agone, but still that nameless paranoid urge had driven him on and on, deeper and deeper into those trackless ways. Kane could not have analysed this call; he would have attributed it to Satan, who lures men to their destruction. But it was but the restless turbulent spirit of the adventurer, the wanderer—the same urge which sends the gipsy caravans about the world, which drove the Viking galleys over unknown seas and which guides the flights of the wild geese.

Kane sighed. Here in this barren land seemed neither food nor water, but he had wearied unto death of the dank, rank venom of the thick jungle. Even a wilderness of bare hills was preferable, for a time at least. He glanced at them, where they lay brooding in the sun, and started forward again.

He held N'Longa's fetish stave in his left hand, and though his conscience still troubled him for keeping a thing so apparently diabolic in nature, he had never been able to bring himself to throw it away.

Now as he went toward the hills, a sudden commotion broke out in the tall grass in front of him, which was, in places, taller than a man. A thin, high-pitched scream sounded and on its heels an earth-shaking roar. The grass parted and a slim figure came flying toward him like a wisp of straw blown on the wind—a brown-skinned girl, clad only in a skirt-like garment. Behind her, some yards away but gaining swiftly, came a huge lion.

The girl fell at Kane's feet with a wail and a sob, and lay clutching at his ankles. The Englishman dropped the voodoo stave, raised his musket to his shoulder and sighted coolly at the ferocious feline face which neared him every instant. Crash! The girl screamed once and slumped on her face. The huge cat leaped high and wildly, to fall and lie motionless.

Kane reloaded hastily before he spared a glance at the form at his feet. The girl lay as still as the lion he had just slain, but a quick examination showed that she had only fainted.

He bathed her face with water from his canteen and presently she opened her eyes and sat up. Fear flooded her face as she looked at her rescuer, and she made to rise.

Kane held out a restraining hand and she cowered down, trembling. The roar of his heavy musket was enough to frighten any native who had never before seen a white man, Kane reflected.

The girl was slim and well-formed. Her nose was straight and thin-bridged. She was a deep brown in colour, perhaps with a strong Berber strain.

Kane spoke to her in a river dialect, a simple language he had learned during his wanderings and she replied haltingly. The inland tribe traded slaves and ivory to the river people and were familiar with their jargon.

"My village is there," she answered Kane's question, pointing to the southern jungle with a slim, rounded arm. "My name is Zunna. My mother whipped me for breaking a cooking-kettle and I ran away because I was angry. I am afraid; let me go back to my mother!"

"You may go," said Kane, "but I will take you, child. Suppose another lion came along? You were very foolish to run away."

She whimpered a little. "Are you not a god?"

"No. Zunna. I am only a man, though the colour of my skin is not as yours. Lead me now to your village."

She rose hesitantly, eyeing him apprehensively through the wild tangle of her hair. To Kane she seemed like some frightened young animal. She led the way and Kane followed. She indicated that her village lay to the southeast, and their route brought them nearer to the hills. The sun began to sink and the roaring of lions reverberated over the grasslands. Kane glanced at the western sky; open country was no place in which to be caught by night. He glanced toward the hills and saw that they were within a few hundred yards of the nearest. He saw what seemed to be a cave.

"Zunna," said he haltingly, "we can never reach your village before nightfall. If we bide here the lions will take us. Yonder is a cavern where we may spend the night—"

She shrank and trembled.

"Not in the hills, master!" she whimpered. "Better the lions!"

"Nonsense!" His tone was impatient; he had had enough of native superstition. "We will spend the night in yonder cave."

She argued no further, but followed him. They went up a short slope and stood at the mouth of the cavern, a small affair, with sides of solid rock and floor of deep sand.

"Gather some dry grass, Zunna," commanded Kane, standing his musket against the wall at the mouth of the cave, "but go not far away, and listen for lions. I will build here a fire which shall keep us safe from beasts tonight. Bring some grass and twigs you may find, like a good child, and we will sup. I have dried meat in my pouch and water also."

She gave him a strange, long glance, then turned away without a word. Kane tore up grass near at hand, noting how it was seared and crisp from the sun, and heaping it up, struck flint and steel. Flame leaped up and devoured the heap in an instant. He was wondering how he could gather enough grass to keep a fire going all night, when he was aware that he had visitors.

Kane was used to grotesque sights, but at first glance he started and a slight coldness travelled down his spine. Two men stood before him in silence. They were tall and gaunt and entirely naked. Their skins were a dusty black, tinged with a grey, ashy hue, as of death. Their faces were different from any he had ever seen. The brows were high and narrow, the noses huge and snout-like; the eyes were inhumanly large and inhumanly red. As the two stood there it seemed to Kane that only their burning eyes lived.

He spoke to them, but they did not answer. He invited them to eat with a motion of his hand, and they silently squatted down near the cave mouth, as far from the dying embers of the fire as they could get.

Kane turned to his pouch and began taking out the strips of dried meat which he carried. Once he glanced at his silent guests; it seemed to him that they were watching the glowing ashes of his fire, rather than him.

The sun was about to sink behind the western horizon. A red, fierce glow spread over the grasslands, so that it seemed like a waving sea of blood. Kane knelt over his pouch, and glancing up, saw Zunna come around the shoulder of the hill with her arms full of grass and dry branches.

As he looked, her eyes flared wide; the branches dropped from her arms and her scream knifed the silence, fraught with terrible warning. Kane whirled on his knee. Two great forms loomed over him as he came up with the lithe motion of a springing leopard. The fetish stave was in his hand and he drove it through the body of the nearest foe with a force which sent its sharp point out between the man's shoulders. Then the long, lean arms of the other locked about him, and the two went down together.

The talon-like nails of the stranger were tearing at his face, the hideous red eyes staring into his with a terrible threat, as Kane writhed about and, fending off the clawing hands with one arm, drew a pistol. He pressed the muzzle close against the savage side and pulled the trigger. At the muffled report, the stranger's body jerked to the concussion of the bullet, but the thick lips merely gaped in a horrid grin.

One long arm slid under Kane's shoulders, the other hand gripped his hair, the Englishman felt his head being forced back irresistibly. He clutched at the other's wrists with both hands, but the flesh under his frantic fingers was as hard as wood. Kane's brain was reeling; his neck seemed ready to break with a little more pressure. He threw his body backward with one volcanic effort, breaking the deadly hold. The other was on him, and the talons were clutching again. Kane found and raised the empty pistol, and he felt the man's skull cave in like a shell as he brought down the long barrel with all his strength. And once again the writhing lips parted in fearful mockery.

And now a near panic clutched Kane. What sort of man was this, who still menaced his life with tearing fingers, after having been shot and mortally bludgeoned? No man, surely, but one of the sons of Satan! At the thought Kane wrenched and heaved explosively, and the close-locked combatants tumbled across the earth to come to a rest in the smouldering ashes before the cave mouth. Kane barely felt the heat, but the mouth of his foe gaped, this time in seeming agony. The frightful fingers loosened their hold and Kane sprang clear.

The savage creature with his shattered skull was rising on one hand and one knee when Kane struck, returning to the attack as a gaunt wolf returns to a wounded bison. From the side he leaped, landing full on the sinewy back, his steely arms seeking and finding a deadly wrestling hold; and as they went to the earth together he broke the other's neck, so that the hideous dead face looked back over one shoulder. The body lay still but to Kane it seemed that it was not dead even then, for the red eyes still burned with their grisly light.

The Englishman turned, to see the girl crouching against the cave wall. He looked for his stave; it lay in a heap of dust, among which were a few mouldering bones. He stared, his brain reeling. Then with one stride he caught up the voodoo staff and turned to the fallen man. His face set in grim lines as he raised it; then he drove it through the savage breast. And before his eyes, the great body crumbled, dissolving to dust as he watched horror-struck, even as the first opponent had crumbled when Kane had first thrust the stave.

III. — DREAM MAGIC

"GREAT GOD!" whispered Kane. "The men were dead! Vampires! This is Satan's handiwork manifested."

Zunna crawled to his knees and clung there.

"These be walking dead men, master," she whimpered. "I should have warned you."

"Why did they not leap on my back when they first came?" asked he.

"They feared the fire. They were waiting for the embers to die entirely."

"Whence came they?"

"From the hills. Hundreds of their kind swarm among the boulders and caverns of these hills, and they live on human life, for a man they will slay, devouring his ghost as it leaves his quivering body. Aye, they are suckers of souls!

"Master, among the greater of these hills there is a silent city of stone, and in the old times, in the days of my ancestors, these people lived there. They were human, but they were not as we, for they had ruled this land for ages and ages. The ancestors of my people made war on them and slew many, and their magicians made all the dead men as these were. At last all died.

"And for ages have they preyed on the tribes of the jungle, stalking down from the hills at mid-night and at sunset to haunt the jungle-ways and slay and slay. Men and beasts flee them and only fire will destroy them."

"Here is that which will destroy them," said Kane grimly, raising the voodoo stave. "Black magic must fight black magic, and I know not what spell N'Longa put hereon, but—"

"You are a god," Zunna decided aloud. "No man could overcome two of the walking dead men. Master, can you not lift this curse from my tribe? There is nowhere for us to flee and the monsters slay us at will, catching wayfarers outside the village wall. Death is on this land and we die helpless!"

Deep in Kane stirred the spirit of the crusader, the fire of the zealot—the fanatic who devotes his life to battling the powers of darkness.

"Let us eat," said he; "then we will build a great fire at the cave mouth. The fire which keeps away beasts shall also keep away fiends."

Later Kane sat just inside the cave, chin rested on clenched fist, eyes gazing unseeingly into the fire. Behind in the shadows, Zunna watched him, awed.

"God of Hosts," Kane muttered, "grant me aid! My hand it is which must lift the ancient curse from this dark land. How am I to fight these dead fiends, who yield not to mortal weapons? Fire will destroy them—a broken neck renders them helpless—the voodoo stave thrust through them crumbles them to dust—but of what avail? How may I prevail against the hundreds who haunt these hills, and to whom human life-essence is Life? Have not—as Zunna says—warriors come against them in the past, only to find them fled to their high-walled city where no man can come against them?"

The night wore on. Zunna slept, her cheek pillowed on her round, girlish arm. The roaring of the lions shook the hills and still Kane sat and gazed broodingly into the fire. Outside, the night was alive with whispers and rustlings and stealthily soft footfalls. And at times Kane, glancing up from his meditations, seemed to catch the gleam of great red eyes beyond the flickering light of the fire.

Grey dawn was stealing over the grasslands when Kane shook Zunna into wakefulness.

"God have mercy on my soul for delving in barbaric magic," said he, "but demonry must be fought with demonry, mayhap. Tend ye the fire and awake me if aught untoward occur."

Kane lay down on his back on the sand floor and laid the voodoo staff on his breast, folding his hands upon it. He fell asleep instantly. And sleeping, he dreamed. To his slumbering self it seemed that he walked through a thick fog and in this fog he met N'Longa, true to life. N'Longa spoke, and the words were clear and vivid, impressing themselves on his consciousness so deeply as to span the gap between sleeping and waking.

"Send this girl to her village soon after sun-up when the lions have gone to their lairs," said N'Longa, "and bid her bring her lover to you at this cave. There make him lie down as if to slumber, holding the voodoo stave."

The dream faded and Kane awoke suddenly, wondering. How strange and vivid had been the vision, and how strange to hear N'Longa talking in English, without the jargon! Kane shrugged his shoulders. He knew that N'Longa claimed to possess the power of sending his spirit through space, and he himself had seen the voodoo man animate a dead man's body. Still—

"Zunna," said Kane, giving the problem up, "I will go with you as far as the edge of the jungle and you must go on to your village and return here to this cave with your lover."

"Kran?" she asked naively.

"Whatever his name is. Eat and we will go."

Again the sun slanted toward the west. Kane sat in the cave, waiting. He had seen the girl safely to the place where the jungle thinned to the grasslands, and though his conscience stung him at the thought of the dangers which might confront her, he sent her on alone and returned to the cave. He sat now, wondering if he would not be damned to everlasting flames for tinkering with the magic of a black sorcerer, blood-brother or not.

Light footfalls sounded, and as Kane reached for his musket, Zunna entered, accompanied by a tall, splendidly proportioned youth whose brown skin showed that he was of the same race as the girl. His soft dreamy eyes were fixed on Kane in a sort of awesome worship. Evidently the girl had not minimized this new god's glory in her telling.

He bade the youth lie down as he directed and placed the voodoo stave in his hands. Zunna crouched at one side, wide-eyed. Kane stepped back, half ashamed of this mummery and wondering what, if anything, would come of it. Then to his horror, the youth gave one gasp and stiffened!

Zunna screamed, bounding erect—"You have killed Kran!" she shrieked, flying at the Englishman who stood struck speechless.

Then she halted suddenly, wavered, drew a hand languidly across her brow—she slid down to lie with her arms about the motionless body of her lover.

And this body moved suddenly, made aimless motions with hands and feet, then sat up, disengaging itself from the clinging arms of the still senseless girl.

Kran looked up at Kane and grinned, a sly, knowing grin which seemed out of place on his face somehow. Kane started. Those soft eyes had changed in expression and were now hard and glittering and snaky—N'Longa's eyes!

"Ai ya," said Kran in a grotesquely familiar voice. "Blood-brother, you got no greeting for N'Longa?"

Kane was silent. His flesh crawled in spite of himself—Kran rose and stretched his arms in an unfamiliar sort of way, as if his limbs were new to him. He slapped his breast approvingly.

"Me N'Longa!" said he in the old boastful manner. "Mighty ju-ju man! Blood-brother, not you know me, eh?"

"You are Satan," said Kane sincerely. "Are you Kran or are you N'Longa?"

"Me N'Longa," assured the other. "My body sleep in ju-ju hut on Coast many treks from here. I borrow Kran's body for while. My ghost travel ten days march in one breath; twenty days march in same time. My ghost go out from my body and drive out Kran's."

"And Kran is dead?"

"No, he no dead. I send his ghost to shadow-land for a while— send the girl's ghost too, to keep him company; bimeby come back."

"This is the work of the Devil," said Kane frankly, "but I have seen you do even fouler magic—shall I call you N'Longa or Kran?"

"Kran—kah! Me N'Longa—bodies like clothes! Me N'Longa, in here now!" he rapped his breast. "Bimeby Kran live along here— then he be Kran and I be N'Longa, same like before. Kran no live along now; N'Longa live along this one fellow body. Blood-brother, I am N'Longa!"

Kane nodded. This was in truth a land of horror and enchantment; anything was possible, even that the thin voice of N'Longa should speak to him from the great chest of Kran, and the snaky eyes of N'Longa should blink at him from the handsome young face of Kran.

"This land I know long time," said N'Longa, getting down to business. "Mighty ju-ju, these dead people! No need to waste one fellow time—I know—I talk to you in sleep. My blood-brother want to kill out these dead fellows, eh?"

"'Tis a thing opposed to nature," said Kane sombrely. "They are known in my land as vampires. I never expected to come upon a whole nation of them."

IV. — THE SILENT CITY

"NOW we find this stone city," said N'Longa.

"Yes? Why not send your ghost out to kill these vampires?" Kane asked idly.

"Ghost got to have one fellow body to work in." N'Longa answered. "Sleep now. Tomorrow we start."

The sun had set; the fire glowed and flickered in the cave mouth. Kane glanced at the still form of the girl, who lay where she had fallen, and prepared himself for slumber.

"Awake me at midnight," he admonished, "and I will watch from then until dawn."

But when N'Longa finally shook his arm, Kane awoke to see the first light of dawn reddening the land.

"Time we start," said the fetish-man.

"But the girl—are you sure she lives?"

"She live, blood-brother."

"Then in God's name, we can not leave her here at the mercy of any prowling fiend who might chance upon her. Or some lion might—"

"No lion come. Vampire scent still linger, mixed with man scent. One fellow lion he no like man scent and he fear the walking dead men. No beast come, and"—lifting the voodoo stave and laying it across the cave entrance—"no dead man come now."

Kane watched him sombrely and without enthusiasm.

"How will that rod safeguard her?"

"That mighty ju-ju," said N'Longa. "You see how one fellow vampire go along dust alongside that stave! No vampire dare touch or come near it. I gave it to you, because outside Vampire Hills one fellow man sometimes meet a corpse walking in jungle when shadows be black. Not all walking dead men be here. And all must suck Life from men—if not, they rot like dead wood."

"Then make many of these rods and arm the people with them."

"No can do!" N'Longa's skull shook violently. "That ju-ju rod be mighty magic! Old, old! No man live today can tell how old that fellow ju-ju stave be. I make my blood-brother sleep and do magic with it to guard him, that time we make palaver in Coast village. Today we scout and run, no need it. Leave it here to guard girl."

Kane shrugged his shoulders and followed the fetish-man, after glancing back at the still shape which lay in the cave. He would never have agreed to leave her so casually, had he not believed in his heart that she was dead. He had touched her, and her flesh was cold.

They went up among the barren hills as the sun was rising. Higher they climbed, up steep clay slopes, winding their way through ravines and between great boulders. The hills were honey-combed with dark, forbidding caves, and these they passed warily, and Kane's flesh crawled as he thought of the grisly occupants therein. For N'Longa said:

"Them vampires, he sleep in caves most all day till sunset. Them caves, he be full of one fellow dead man."

The sun rose higher, baking down on the bare slopes with an intolerable heat. Silence brooded like an evil monster over the land. They had seen nothing, but Kane could have sworn at times that a black shadow drifted behind a boulder at their approach.

"Them vampires, they stay hid in daytime." said N'Longa with a low laugh. "They be afraid of one fellow vulture! No fool vulture! He know death when he see it! He pounce on one fellow dead man and tear and eat if he be lying or walking!"

A strong shudder shook his companion.

"Great God!" Kane cried, striking his thigh with his hat; "is there no end to the horror of this hideous land? Truly this land is dedicated to the powers of darkness!"

Kane's eyes burned with a dangerous light. The terrible heat, the solitude and the knowledge of the horrors lurking on either hand were shaking even his steely nerves.

"Keep on one fellow hat, blood-brother," admonished N'Longa with a low gurgle of amusement. "That fellow sun, he knock you dead, suppose you no look out."

Kane shifted the musket he had insisted on bringing and made no reply. They mounted an eminence at last and looked down on a sort of plateau. And in the centre of this plateau was a silent city of grey and crumbling stone. Kane was smitten by a sense of incredible age as he looked. The walls and houses were of great stone blocks, yet they were falling into ruin. Grass grew on the plateau, and high in the streets of that dead city. Kane saw no movement among the ruins.

"That is their city—why do they choose to sleep in the caves?"

"Maybe-so one fellow stone fall on them from roof and crush. Them stone huts, he fall down bimeby. Maybe-so they no like to stay together—maybe-so they eat each other, too."

"Silence!" whispered Kane; "how it hangs over all!"

"Them vampires no talk nor yell; they dead. They sleep in caves, wander at sunset and at night. Maybe-so them fellow bush tribes come with spears, them vampires go to stone kraal and fight behind walls."

Kane nodded. The crumbling walls which surrounded that dead city were still high and solid enough to resist the attack of spearmen—especially when defended by these snout-nosed fiends.

"Blood-brother," said N'Longa solemnly, "I have mighty magic thought! Be silent a little while."

Kane seated himself on a boulder, and gazed broodingly at the bare crags and slopes which surrounded them. Far away to the south he saw the leafy green ocean that was the jungle. Distance lent a certain enchantment to the scene. Closer at hand loomed the dark blotches that were the mouths of the caves of horror.

N'Longa was squatting, tracing some strange pattern in the clay with a dagger point. Kane watched him, thinking how easy they might fall victim to the vampires if even three or four of the fiends should come out of their caverns. And even as he thought it, a black and horrific shadow fell across the crouching fetish-man.

Kane acted without conscious thought. He shot from the boulder where he sat—like a stone hurled from a catapult, and his musket stock shattered the face of the hideous thing who had stolen upon them. Back and back Kane drove his inhuman foe staggering, never giving him time to halt or launch an offensive, battering him with the onslaught of a frenzied tiger.

At the very edge of the cliff the vampire wavered, then pitched back over, to fall for a hundred feet and lie writhing on the rocks of the plateau below. N'Longa was on his feet pointing; the hills were giving up their dead.

Out of the caves they were swarming, the terrible black silent shapes; up the slopes they came charging and over the boulders they came clambering, and their red eyes were all turned toward the two humans who stood above the silent city. The caves belched them forth in an unholy judgment day.

N'Longa pointed to a crag some distance away and with a shout started running fleetly toward it. Kane followed. From behind boulders taloned hands clawed at them, tearing their garments. They raced past caves, and mummied monsters came lurching out of the dark, gibbering silently, to join in the pursuit.

The dead hands were close at their back when they scrambled up the last slope and stood on a ledge which was the top of the crag. The fiends halted silently a moment, then came clambering after them. Kane clubbed his musket and smashed down into the red-eyed faces, knocking aside the upleaping hands. They surged up like a great wave; he swung his musket in a silent fury that matched theirs. The wave broke and wavered back, then came on again.

He—could—not—kill—them! These words beat on his brain like a sledge on an anvil as he shattered wood-like flesh and dead bone with his smashing swings. He knocked them down, hurled them back, but they rose and came on again. This could not last—what in God's name was N'Longa doing? Kane spared one swift, tortured glance over his shoulder. The fetish-man stood on the highest part of the ledge, head thrown back, arms lifted as if in invocation.

Kane's vision blurred to the sweep of hideous faces with red, staring eyes. Those in front were horrible to see now, for their skulls were shattered, their faces caved in and their limbs broken. But still they came on and those behind reached across their shoulders to clutch at the man who defied them.

Kane was red but the blood was all his. From the long-withered veins of those monsters no single drop of warm red blood trickled. Suddenly from behind him came a long piercing wall— from N'Longa! Over the crash of the flying musket-stock and the shattering of bones it sounded high and clear—the only voice lifted in that hideous fight.

The wave of vampires washed about Kane's feet, dragging him down. Keen talons tore at him, flaccid lips sucked at his wounds. He reeled up again, dishevelled and bloody, clearing a space with a shattering sweep of his splintered musket. Then they closed in again and he went down.

"This is the end!" he thought, but even at that instant the press slackened and the sky was suddenly filled with the beat of great wings.

Then he was free and staggered up, blindly and dizzily, ready to renew the strife. He halted, frozen. Down the slope the vampire horde was fleeing and over their heads and close at their shoulders flew huge vultures, tearing and rending avidly, sinking their beaks in the dead flesh, devouring the creatures as they fled.

Kane laughed, almost insanely.

"Defy man and God, but you may not deceive the vultures, sons of Satan! They know whether a man be alive or dead!"

N'Longa stood like a prophet on the pinnacle, and the great black birds soared and wheeled about him. His arms still waved and his voice still wailed out across the hills. And over the skylines they came, hordes on endless hordes—vultures, vultures, vultures! come to the feast so long denied them. They blackened the sky with their numbers, blotted out the sun; a strange darkness fell on the land. They settled in long dusky lines, diving into the caverns with a whir of wings and a clash of beaks. Their talons tore at the evil horrors which these caves disgorged.

Now all the vampires were fleeing to their city. The vengeance held back for ages had come down on them and their last hope was the heavy walls which had kept back the desperate human foes. Under those crumbling roofs they might find shelter. And N'Longa watched them stream into the city, and he laughed until the crags re-echoed.

Now all were in and the birds settled like a cloud over the doomed city, perching in solid rows along the walls, sharpening their beaks and claws on the towers.

And N'Longa struck flint and steel to a bundle of dry leaves he had brought with him. The bundle leaped into instant flame and he straightened and flung the blazing thing far out over the cliffs. It fell like a meteor to the plateau beneath, showering sparks. The tall grass of the plateau leaped aflame.

From the silent city beneath them, fear flowed in unseen waves, like a white fog. Kane smiled grimly.

"The grass is sere and brittle from the drought," he said; "there has been even less rain than usual this season; it will burn swiftly."

Like a crimson serpent the fire ran through high dead grass. It spread and it spread and Kane, standing high above, yet felt the fearful intensity of the hundreds of red eyes which watched from the stone city.

Now the scarlet snake had reached the walls and was rearing as if to coil and writhe over them. The vultures rose on heavily flapping wings and soared reluctantly. A vagrant gust of wind whipped the blaze about and drove it in a long red sheet around the wall. Now the city was hemmed in on all sides by a solid barricade of flame. The roar came up to the two men on the high crag.

Sparks flew across the wall, lighting in the high grass in the streets. A score of flames leaped up and grew with terrifying speed. A veil of red cloaked streets and buildings, and through this crimson, whirling mist Kane and N'Longa saw hundreds of dark shapes scamper and writhe, to vanish suddenly in red bursts of flame. There rose an intolerable scent of decayed flesh burning.

Kane gazed, awed. This was truly a hell on earth. As in a nightmare he looked into the roaring red cauldron where dark insects fought against their doom and perished. The flames leaped a hundred feet into the air, and suddenly above their roar sounded one bestial, inhuman scream like a shriek from across nameless gulfs of cosmic apace, as one vampire, dying, broke the chains of silence which had held him for untold centuries. High and haunting it rose, the death cry of a vanishing race.

Then the flames dropped suddenly. The conflagration had been a typical grass fire, short and fierce. Now the plateau showed a blackened expanse and the city a charred and smoking mass of crumbling stone. Not one corpse lay in view, not even a charred bone. Above all whirled the dark swarms of the vultures, but they, too, were beginning to scatter.

Kane gazed hungrily at the clean blue sky. Like a strong sea wind clearing a fog of horror was the sight to him. From somewhere sounded the faint and far-off roaring of a distant lion. The vultures were flapping away in black, straggling lines.

V. — PALAVER SET!

KANE sat in the mouth of the cave where Zunna lay, submitting to the fetish-man's bandaging.

The Puritan's garments hung in tatters about his frame; his limbs and breast were deeply gashed and darkly bruised, but he had had no mortal wound in that deathly fight on the cliff.

"Mighty men, we be!" declared N'Longa with deep approval. "Vampire city be silent now, sure 'nough! No walking dead man live along these hills."

"I do not understand," said Kane, resting chin on hand. "Tell me, N'Longa, how have you done things? How talked you with me in my dreams; how came you into the body of Kran; and how summoned you the vultures?"

"My blood-brother," said N'Longa, discarding his pride in his pidgin English, to drop into the river language understood by

Kane, "I am so old that you would call me a liar if I told you my age. All my life I have worked magic, sitting first at the feet of mighty ju-ju men of the south and the east; then I was a slave to the Buckra and learned more. My brother, shall I span all these years in a moment and make you understand with a word, what has taken me so long to learn? I could not even make you understand how these vampires have kept their bodies from decay by drinking the lives of men.

"I sleep and my spirit goes out over the jungle and the rivers to talk with the sleeping spirits of my friends. There is a mighty magic on the voodoo staff I gave you—a magic out of the Old Land which draws my ghost to it as a white man's magnet draws metal."

Kane listened unspeaking, seeing for the first time in N'Longa's glittering eyes something stronger and deeper than the avid gleam of the worker in black magic. To Kane it seemed almost as if he looked into the far-seeing and mystic eyes of a prophet of old.

"I spoke to you in dreams," N'Longa went on, "and I made a deep sleep come over the souls of Kran and of Zunna, and removed them to a far dim land, whence they shall soon return, unremembering. All things bow to magic, blood-brother, and beasts and birds obey the master words. I worked strong voodoo, vulture-magic, and flying people of the air gathered at my call."

"These things I know and am a part of, but how shall I tell you of them? Blood-brother, you are a mighty warrior, but in the ways of magic you are as a little child lost. And what has taken me long dark years to know, I may not divulge to you so you would understand. My friend, you think only of bad spirits, but were my magic always bad, should I not take this fine young body in place of my old wrinkled one and keep it? But Kran shall have his body back safely."

"Keep the voodoo staff, blood-brother. It has mighty power against all sorcerers and serpents and evil things. Now I return to the village on the Coast where my true body sleeps. And what of you, my blood-brother?"

Kane pointed silently eastward.

"The call grows no weaker. I go."

N'Longa nodded, held out his hand. Kane grasped it. The mystical expression had gone from the fetish-man's face and the eyes twinkled snakily with a sort of reptilian mirth.

"Me go now, blood-brother," said the fetish-man, returning to his beloved jargon, of which knowledge he was prouder than all his conjuring tricks. "You take care—that one fellow jungle, she pluck your bones yet! Remember that voodoo stave, brother. Ai ya, palaver set!"

He fell back on the sand, and Kane saw the keen, sly expression of N'Longa fading from the face of Kran. His flesh crawled again. Somewhere back on the Slave Coast, the body of N'Longa, withered and wrinkled, was stirring in the ju-ju hut, was rising as if from a deep sleep. Kane shuddered.

Kran sat up, yawned, stretched and smiled. Beside him the girl Zunna rose, rubbing her eyes.

"Master," said Kran apologetically, "we must have slumbered."

The Footfalls Within (*Robert E. Howard*)

SOLOMON KANE gazed sombrely at the native woman who lay dead at his feet. Little more than a girl she was, but her wasted limbs and staring eyes showed that she had suffered much before death brought her merciful relief. Kane noted the chain galls on her limbs, the deep crisscrossed scars on her back, the mark of the yoke on her neck. His cold eyes deepened strangely, showing chill glints and lights like clouds passing across depths of ice.

"Even into this lonesome land they come," he muttered. "I had not thought—"

He raised his head and gazed eastward. Black dots against the blue wheeled and circled.

"The kites mark their trail," muttered the tall Englishman. "Destruction goeth before them and death followeth after. Woe unto ye, sons of iniquity, for the wrath of God is upon ye. The cords be loosed on the iron necks of the hounds of hate and the bow of vengeance is strung. Ye are proud-stomached and strong, and the people cry out beneath your feet, but retribution cometh in the blackness of midnight and the redness of dawn." He shifted the belt that held his heavy pistols and the keen dirk, instinctively touched the long rapier at his hip, and went stealthily but swiftly eastward. A cruel anger burned in his deep eyes like blue volcanic fires burning beneath leagues of ice, and the hand that gripped his long, cat-headed stave hardened into iron.

After some hours of steady striding, he came within hearing of the slave train that wound its laborious way through the jungle. The piteous cries of the slaves, the shouts and curses of the drivers, and the cracking of the whips came plainly to his ears. Another hour brought him even with them, and gliding along through the jungle parallel to the trail taken by the slavers, he spied upon them safely. Kane had fought Indians in Darien and had learned much of their woodcraft.

More than a hundred natives, young men and women, staggered along the trail, stark naked and made fast together by cruel yoke-like affairs of wood. These yokes, rough and heavy, fitted over their necks and linked them together, two by two. The yokes were in turn fettered together, making one long chain. Of the drivers there were fifteen Arabs and some seventy negro warriors, whose weapons and fantastic apparel showed them to be of some eastern tribe—one of those tribes subjugated and made Moslems and allies by the conquering Arabs.

Five Arabs walked ahead of the train with some thirty of their warriors, and five brought up the rear with the rest of the negro warriors. The rest marched beside the staggering slaves, urging them along with shouts and curses and with long, cruel whips which brought spurts of blood at almost every blow. These slavers were fools as well as rogues, reflected Kane—not more than half of them would survive the hardships of the trek to the coast.

He wondered at the presence of these raiders, for this country lay far to the south of the districts which they usually frequented. But avarice can drive men far, as the Englishman knew. He had dealt with these gentry of old. Even as he watched, old scars burned in his back—scars made by Moslem whips in a Turkish galley. And deeper still burned Kane's unquenchable hate.

The Puritan followed, shadowing his foes like a ghost, and as he stole through the jungle, he racked his brain for a plan. How might he prevail against that horde? All of the Arabs and many of their allies were armed with guns—long, clumsy firelock affairs, it is true, but guns just the same, enough to awe any tribe of natives who might oppose them. Some carried in their wide girdles long, silver-chased pistols of more effective pattern—flintlocks of Moorish and Turkish make.

Kane followed like a brooding ghost and his rage and hatred ate into his soul like a canker. Each crack of the whips was like a blow on his own shoulders. The heat and cruelty of the tropics play queer tricks. Ordinary passions become monstrous things; irritation runs to a berserker rage; anger flames into unexpected madness and men kill in a red mist of passion, and wonder, aghast, afterward. The fury Solomon Kane felt would have been enough at any time and in any place to shake a man to his foundation. Now it assumed monstrous proportions, so that Kane shivered as if with a chill; iron claws scratched at his brain and he saw the slaves and the slavers through a crimson mist. Yet he might not have put his hate-born insanity into action had it not been for a mishap.

One of the slaves, a slim young girl, suddenly faltered and slipped to the earth, dragging her yoke-mate with her. A tall, hook-nosed Arab yelled savagely and lashed her viciously. Her yoke-mate staggered partly up, but the girl remained prone, writhing weakly beneath the lash but evidently unable to rise. She whimpered pitifully between her parched lips, and other slavers came about her, their whips descending on her quivering flesh in slashes of red agony.

A half hour of rest and a little water would have revived her, but the Arabs had no time to spare. Solomon, biting his arm until his teeth met in the flesh as he fought for control, thanked God that the lashing had ceased and steeled himself for the swift flash of the dagger that would put the child beyond torment. But the Arabs were in a mood for sport. Since the girl would fetch them no profit on the market block, they would utilize her for their pleasure—and their humour was such as to turn men's blood to icy water.

A shout from the first whipper brought the rest crowding around, their bearded faces split in grins of delighted anticipation, while their savage allies edged nearer, their eyes gleaming. The wretched slaves realized their masters' intentions and a chorus of pitiful cries rose from them.

Kane, sick with horror, realized, too, that the girl's was to be no easy death. He knew what the tall Moslem intended to do, as he stooped over her with a keen dagger such as the Arabs used for skinning game. Madness overcame the Englishman. He valued his own life little; he had risked it without thought for the sake of a pagan child or a small animal. Yet he would not have premeditatedly thrown away his one hope of succouring the wretches in the train. But he acted without conscious thought. A pistol was smoking in his hand and the tall butcher was down in the dust of the trail with his brains oozing out, before Kane realized what he had done.

He was almost as astonished as the Arabs, who stood frozen for a moment and then burst into a medley of yells. Several threw up their clumsy firelocks and sent their heavy balls crashing through the trees, and the rest, thinking no doubt that they were ambushed, led a reckless charge into the jungle. The bold suddenness of that move was Kane's undoing. Had they hesitated a moment longer he might have faded away unobserved, but as it was he saw no choice but to meet them openly and sell his life as highly as he could.

And indeed it was with a certain ferocious fascination that he faced his howling attackers. They halted in sudden amazement as the tall, grim Englishman stepped from behind his tree, and in that instant one of them died with a bullet from Kane's remaining pistol in his heart. Then with yells of savage rage they flung themselves on their lone defier.

Solomon Kane placed his back against a huge tree and his long rapier played a shining wheel about him. An Arab and three of his equally fiercer allies were hacking at him with their heavy curved blades while the rest milled about, snarling like wolves, as they sought to drive in blade or ball without maiming one of their own number.

The flickering rapier parried the whistling scimitars and the Arab died on its point, which seemed to hesitate in his heart only an instant before it pierced the brain of a sword-wielding warrior. Another attacker dropped his sword and leaped in to grapple at close quarters. He was disembowelled by the dirk in Kane's left hand, and the others gave back in sudden fear. A heavy ball smashed against the tree close to Kane's head and he tensed himself to spring and die in the thick of them. Then their sheikh lashed them on with his long whip, and Kane heard him shouting fiercely for his warriors to take the infidel alive. Kane answered the command with a sudden cast of his dirk, which hummed so close to the sheikh's head that it slit his turban and sank deep in the shoulder of one behind him.

The sheikh drew his silver-chased pistols, threatening his own men with death if they did not take this fierce opponent, and they charged in again desperately. One of the warriors ran full upon Kane's sword and an Arab behind the fellow, with ruthless craft, thrust the screaming wretch suddenly forward on the weapon, driving it hilt-deep in his writhing body, fouling the blade. Before Kane could wrench it clear, with a yell of triumph the pack rushed in on him and bore him down by sheer weight of numbers. As they grappled him from all sides, the Puritan wished in vain for the dirk he had thrown away. But even so, his taking was none too easy.

Blood spattered and faces caved in beneath his iron-hard fists that splintered teeth and shattered bone. A warrior reeled away disabled from a vicious drive of knee to groin. Even when they had him stretched out and piled man-weight on him, until he could no longer strike with fists or foot, his long lean fingers sank fiercely through a matted beard to lock about a corded throat in a grip that took the power of three strong men to break and left the victim gasping and green-faced.

At last, panting from the terrific struggle, they had him bound hand and foot and the sheikh, thrusting his pistols back into his silken sash, came striding to stand and look down at his captive. Kane glared up at the tall, lean frame, at the hawk-like face with its black-curled beard and arrogant brown eyes.

"I am the sheikh Hassim ben Said," said the Arab. "Who are you?"

"My name is Solomon Kane," growled the Puritan in the sheikh's own language. "I am an Englishman, you heathen jackal."

The dark eyes of the Arab flickered with interest.

"Suleiman Kahani," said he, giving the Arabesque equivalent of the English name. "I have heard of you—you have fought the Turks betimes and the Barbary corsairs have licked their wounds because of you." Kane deigned no reply. Hassim shrugged his shoulders.

"You will bring a fine price," said he. "Mayhap I will take you to Stamboul, where there are Shahs who would desire such a man among their slaves. And I mind me now of one Kemal Bey, a man of ships, who wears a deep scar across his face of your making and who curses the name of Englishman. He will pay me a high price for you. And behold, oh Frank, I do you the honour of appointing you a separate guard. You shall not walk in the yoke-chain but free save for your hands."

Kane made no answer, and at a sign from the sheikh, he was hauled to his feet and his bonds loosened except for his hands, which they left bound firmly behind him. A stout cord was looped about his neck and the other end of this was given into the hand of a huge warrior who bore in his free hand a great curved scimitar.

"And now what think ye of my favour to you, Frank?" queried the sheikh.

"I am thinking," answered Kane in a slow, deep voice of menace, "that I would trade my soul's salvation to face you and your sword, alone and unarmed, and to tear the heart from your breast with my naked fingers."

Such was the concentrated hate in his deep resounding voice, and such primal, unconquerable fury blazed from his terrible eyes, that the hardened and fearless chieftain blanched and involuntarily recoiled as if from a maddened beast.

Then Hassim recovered his poise and with a short word to his followers, strode to the head of the cavalcade. Kane noted with thankfulness that the respite occasioned by his capture had given the girl who had fallen a chance to rest and revive. The skinning knife had not had time to more than touch her; she was able to reel along. Night was not far away. Soon the slavers would be forced to halt and camp.

The Englishman perforce took up the trek, his guard remaining a few paces behind with a huge blade ever ready. Kane also noted with a touch of grim vanity, that three more warriors marched close behind, muskets ready and matches burning. They had tasted his prowess and they were taking no chances. His weapons had been recovered and Hassim had promptly appropriated all except the cat-headed ju-ju stave. This had been contemptuously cast aside by him and taken up by one of the savage warriors.

The Englishman was presently aware that a lean, grey-bearded Arab was walking along at his side. This Arab seemed desirous of speaking but strangely timid, and the source of his timidity seemed, curiously enough, the ju-ju stave which he had taken from the man who had picked it up, and which he now turned uncertainly in his hands.

"I am Yussef the Hadji," said this Arab suddenly. "I have naught against you. I had no hand in attacking you and would be your friend if you would let me. Tell me, Frank, whence comes this staff and how comes it into your hands?"

Kane's first inclination was to consign his questioner to the infernal regions, but a certain sincerity of manner in the old man made him change his mind and he answered: "It was given me by my blood-brother—a magician of the Slave Coast, named N'Longa."

The old Arab nodded and muttered in his beard and presently sent a warrior running forward to bid Hassim return. The tall sheikh presently came striding back along the slow-moving column, with a clank and jingle of daggers and sabres, with Kane's dirk and pistols thrust into his wide sash.

"Look, Hassim," the old Arab thrust forward the stave, "you cast it away without knowing what you did!"

"And what of it?" growled the sheikh. "I see naught but a staff—sharp-pointed and with the head of a cat on the other end—a staff with strange infidel carvings upon it."

The older man shook it at him in excitement: "This staff is older than the world! It holds mighty magic! I have read of it in the old iron-bound books and Mohammed—on whom peace!—himself hath spoken of it by allegory and parable! See the cat-head upon it? It is the head of a goddess of ancient Egypt! Ages ago, before Mohammed taught, before Jerusalem was, the priests of Bast bore this rod before the bowing, chanting worshippers! With it Musa did wonders before Pharaoh and when the Yahudi fled from Egypt they bore it with them. And for centuries it was the sceptre of Israel and Judah and with it Suleiman ben Daoud drove forth the conjurers and magicians and prisoned the efreets and the evil genii! Look! Again in the hands of a Suleiman we find the ancient rod!"

Old Yussef had worked himself into a pitch of almost fanatic fervour but Hassim merely shrugged his shoulders.

"It did not save the Jews from bondage nor this Suleiman from our captivity," said he. "I value it not as much as I esteem the long thin blade with which he loosed the souls of three of my best swordsmen."

Yussef shook his head. "Your mockery will bring you to no good end, Hassim. Some day you will meet a power that will not divide before your sword or fall to your bullets. I will keep the staff, and I warn you—abuse not the Frank. He has borne the holy and terrible staff of Suleiman and Musa and the Pharaohs, and who knows what magic he has drawn there from? For it is older than the world and has known the terrible hands of strange pre-Adamite priests in the silent cities beneath the seas, and has drawn from an Elder World mystery and magic unguessed by humankind. There were strange kings and stranger priests when the dawns were young, and evil was, even in their day. And with this staff they fought the evil which was ancient when their strange world was young, so many millions of years ago that a man would shudder to count them." Hassim answered impatiently and strode away with old Yussef following him persistently and chattering away in a querulous tone. Kane shrugged his mighty shoulders. With what he knew of the strange powers of that strange staff, he was not one to question the old man's assertions, fantastic as they seemed.

This much he knew—that it was made of a wood that existed nowhere on earth today. It needed but the proof of sight and touch to realize that its material had grown in some world apart. The exquisite workmanship of the head, of a pre-pyramidal age, and the hieroglyphics, symbols of a language that was forgotten when Rome was young—these, Kane sensed, were additions as modern to the antiquity of the staff itself as would be English words carved on the stone monoliths of Stonehenge.

As for the cat-head—looking at it sometimes Kane had a peculiar feeling of alteration; a faint sensing that once the pommel of the staff was carved with a different design. The dust-ancient Egyptian who had carved the head of Bast had merely altered the original figure, and what that figure had been, Kane had never tried to guess. A close scrutiny of the staff always aroused a disquieting and almost dizzy suggestion of abysses of aeons, unprovocative to further speculation.

The day wore on. The sun beat down mercilessly, then screened itself in the great trees as it slanted toward the horizon. The slaves suffered fiercely for water and a continual whimpering rose from their ranks as they staggered blindly on. Some fell and half-crawled, and were half-dragged by their reeling yoke-mates. When all were buckling from exhaustion, the sun dipped, night rushed on, and a halt was called. Camp was pitched, guards thrown out. The slaves were fed scantily and given enough water to keep life in them—but only just enough. Their fetters were not loosened, but they were allowed to sprawl about as they might. Their fearful thirst and hunger having been somewhat eased, they bore the discomforts of their shackles with characteristic stoicism.

Kane was fed without his hands being untied, and he was given all the water he wished. The patient eyes of the slaves watched him drink, silently, and he was sorely ashamed to guzzle what others suffered for; he ceased before his thirst was fully quenched. A wide clearing had been selected, on all sides of which rose gigantic trees. After the Arabs had eaten and while the black Moslems were still cooking their food, old Yussef came to Kane and began to talk about the staff again. Kane answered his questions with admirable patience, considering the hatred he bore the whole race to which the Hadji belonged, and during the conversation, Hassim came striding up and looked down in contempt. Hassim, Kane ruminated, was the very symbol of militant Islam—bold, reckless, materialistic, sparing nothing, fearing nothing, as sure of his own destiny and as contemptuous of the rights of others as the most powerful Western king. "Are you maundering about that stick again?" he gibed. "Hadji, you grow childish in your old age." Yussef's beard quivered in anger. He shook the staff at his sheikh like a threat of evil.

"Your mockery little befits your rank, Hassim," he snapped. "We are in the heart of a dark and demon-haunted land, to which long ago were banished the devils from Arabia; if this staff, which any but a fool can tell is no rod of any world we know, has existed down to our day, who knows what other things, tangible or intangible, may have existed through the ages? This very trail we follow—know you how old it is? Men followed it before the Seljuk came out of the East or the Roman came out of the West. Over this very trail, legends say, the great Suleiman came when he drove the demons westward out of Asia and prisoned them in strange prisons. And will you say—"

A wild shout interrupted him. Out of the shadows of the jungle a warrior came flying as if from the hounds of Doom. With arms flinging wildly, eyes rolling to display the whites, and mouth wide open so that all his gleaming teeth were visible, he made an image of stark terror not soon forgotten. The Moslem horde leaped up, snatching their weapons, and Hassim swore:

"That's Ali, whom I sent to scout for meat—perchance a lion—"

But no lion followed the man who fell at Hassim's feet, mouthing gibberish and pointing wildly back at the black jungle whence the nerve-strung watchers expected some brain-shattering horror to burst. "He says he found a strange mausoleum back in the jungle," said Hassim with a scowl, "but he cannot tell what frightened him. He only knows a great horror overwhelmed him and sent him flying. Ali, you are a fool and a rogue."

He kicked the grovelling savage viciously, but the other Arabs drew about him in some uncertainty. The panic was spreading among the native warriors.

"They will bolt in spite of us," muttered a bearded Arab, uneasily watching the native allies who, milled together, jabbered excitedly and flung fearsome glances over the shoulders. "Hassim, 'twere better to march on a few miles. This is an evil place after all, and though 'tis likely the fool, Ali, was frighted by his own shadow—still—"

"Still," jeered the sheikh, "you will all feel better when we have left it behind. Good enough; to still your fears I will move camp— but first I will have a look at this thing. Lash up the slaves; we'll swing into the jungle and pass by this mausoleum; perhaps some great king lies there. No one will be afraid if we all go in a body with guns."

So the weary slaves were whipped into wakefulness and stumbled along beneath the whips again. The native allies went silently and nervously, reluctantly obeying Hassim's implacable will but huddling close to the Arabs. The moon had risen, huge, red and sullen, and the jungle was bathed in a sinister silver glow that etched the brooding trees in black shadow. The trembling Ali pointed out the way, somewhat reassured by his savage master's presence. And so they passed through the jungle until they came to a strange clearing among the giant trees— strange because nothing grew there. The trees ringed it in a disquieting symmetrical manner, and no lichen or moss grew on the earth, which seemed to have been blasted and blighted in a strange fashion. And in the midst of the glade stood the mausoleum.

A great brooding mass of stone it was, pregnant with ancient evil. Dead with the dead of a hundred centuries it seemed, yet Kane was aware that the air pulsed about it, as with the slow, unhuman breathing of some gigantic, invisible monster.

The Arab's native allies drew back muttering, assailed by the evil atmosphere of the place; the slaves stood in a patient, silent group beneath the trees. The Arabs went forward to the frowning black mass, and Yussef, taking Kane's cord from his guard, led the Englishman with him like a surly mastiff, as if for protection against the unknown.

"Some mighty sultan doubtless lies here," said Hassim, tapping the stone with his scabbard.

"Whence come these stones?" muttered Yussef uneasily. "They are of dark and forbidding aspect. Why should a great sultan lie in state so far from any habitation of man? If there were ruins of an old city hereabouts it would be different—"

He bent to examine the heavy metal door with its huge lock, curiously sealed and fused. He shook his head forebodingly as he made out the ancient Hebraic characters carved on the door.

"I can not read them," he quavered, "and belike it is well for me I can not. What ancient kings sealed up is not good for men to disturb. Hassim, let us hence. This place is pregnant with evil for the sons of men."

But Hassim gave him no heed. "He who lies within is no son of Islam," said he, "and why should we not despoil him of the gems and riches that undoubtedly were laid to rest with him? Let us break open this door."

Some of the Arabs shook their heads doubtfully but Hassim's word was law. Calling to him a huge warrior who bore a heavy hammer, he ordered him to break open the door.

As the man swung up his sledge, Kane gave a sharp exclamation. Was he mad? The apparent antiquity of this brooding mass of stone was proof that it had stood undisturbed for thousands of years. Yet he could have sworn that he heard the sounds of footfalls within! Back and forth they padded, as if something paced the narrow confines of that grisly prison in a never-ending monotony of movement.

A cold hand touched the spine of Solomon Kane. Whether the sounds registered on his conscious ear or on some unsounded deep of soul or sub-feeling, he could not tell, but he knew that somewhere within his consciousness there reechoed the tramp of monstrous feet from within that ghastly mausoleum.

"Stop!" he exclaimed. "Hassim, I may be mad, but I hear the tread of some fiend within that pile of stone." Hassim raised his hand and checked the hovering hammer. He listened intently, and the others strained their ears in a silence that had suddenly become tense.

"I hear nothing," grunted a bearded giant, "Nor I," came a quick chorus. "The Frank is mad!"

"Hear ye anything, Yussef?" asked Hassim sardonically.

The old Hadji shifted nervously. His face was uneasy.

"No. Hassim, no, yet—"

Kane decided he must be mad. Yet in his heart he knew he was never saner, and he knew somehow that this occult keenness of the deeper senses that set him apart from the Arabs came from long association with the ju-ju stave that old Yussef now held in his shaking hands.

Hassim laughed harshly and made a gesture to the warrior. The hammer fell with a crash that re-echoed deafeningly and shivered off through the black jungle in a strangely altered cachinnation. Again—again—and again the hammer fell, driven with all the power of rippling muscles and mighty body. And between the blows Kane still heard that lumbering tread, and he who had never known fear as men know it, felt the cold hand of terror clutching at his heart. This fear was apart from earthly or mortal fear, as the sound of the footfalls was apart from mortal tread. Kane's fright was like a cold wind blowing on him from outer realms of unguessed Darkness, bearing him the evil and decay of an outlived epoch and an unutterably ancient period. Kane was not sure whether he heard those footfalls or by some dim instinct sensed them. But he was sure of their reality. They were not the tramp of man or beast; but inside that black, hideously ancient mausoleum some nameless thing moved with floor-shaking and elephantine tread.

The powerful warrior sweated and panted with the difficulty of his task. But at last, beneath the heavy blows the ancient lock shattered; the hinges snapped; the door burst inward. And Yussef screamed.

From that black gaping entrance no tiger-fanged beast or demon of solid flesh and blood leaped forth. But a fearful stench flowed out in billowing, almost tangible waves and in one brain-shattering, ravening rush, whereby the gaping door seemed to gush blood, the Horror was upon them. It enveloped Hassim, and the fearless chieftain, hewing vainly at the almost intangible terror, screamed with sudden, unaccustomed fright as his lashing scimitar whistled only through stuff as yielding and unharmable as air, and he felt himself lapped by coils of death and destruction.

Yussef shrieked like a lost soul, dropped the ju-ju stave and joined his fellows who streamed out into the jungle in mad flight, preceded by their howling allies. Only the slaves fled not, but stood shackled to their doom, wailing their terror. As in a nightmare of delirium Kane saw Hassim swaying like a reed in the wind, lapped about by a gigantic pulsing red Thing that had neither shape nor earthly substance. Then, as the crack of splintering bones came to him, and the sheikh's body buckled like a straw beneath a stamping hoof, the Englishman burst his bonds with one volcanic effort and caught up the ju-ju stave.

Hassim was down, crushed and dead, sprawled like a broken toy with shattered limbs awry, and the red pulsing Thing was lurching toward Kane like a thick cloud of blood in the air, that continually changed its shape and form, and yet somehow trod lumberingly as if on monstrous legs!

Kane felt the cold fingers of fear claw at his brain, but he braced himself, and lifting the ancient staff, struck with all his power into the centre of the Horror. And he felt an unnameable, immaterial substance meet and give way before the falling staff. Then he was almost strangled by the nauseous burst of unholy stench that flooded the air, and somewhere down the dim vistas of his soul's consciousness re-echoed unbearably a hideous formless cataclysm that he knew was the death-screaming of the monster. For it was down and dying at his feet, its crimson paling in slow surges like the rise and receding of red waves on some foul coast. And as it paled, the soundless screaming dwindled away into cosmic distances as though it faded into some sphere apart and aloof beyond human ken.

Kane, dazed and incredulous, looked down on a shapeless, colourless, all but invisible mass at his feet which he knew was the corpse of the Horror, dashed back into the black realms from whence it had come, by a single blow of the staff of Solomon. Aye, the same staff, Kane knew, that in the hands of a mighty King and magician had ages ago driven the monster into that strange prison, to bide until ignorant hands loosed it again upon the world.

The old tales were true then, and King Solomon had in truth driven the demons westward and sealed them in strange places. Why had he let them live? Was human magic too weak in those dim days to more than subdue the devils? Kane shrugged his shoulders in wonderment. He knew nothing of magic, yet he had slain where that other Solomon had but imprisoned.

And Solomon Kane shuddered, for he had looked on Life that was not Life as he knew it, and had dealt and witnessed Death that was not Death as he knew it. Again the realization swept over him—as it had in the dust-haunted halls of Atlantean Negari, as it had in the abhorrent Hills of the Dead, as it had in Akaana—that human life was but one of a myriad forms of existence, that worlds existed within worlds, and that there was more than one plane of existence. The planet men call the earth spun on through the untold ages, Kane realized, and as it spun it spawned Life, and living things which wriggled about it as maggots are spawned in rot and corruption. Man was the dominant maggot now; why should he in his pride suppose that he and his adjuncts were the first maggots—or the last to rule a planet quick with unguessed life. He shook his head, gazing in new wonder at the ancient gift of N'Longa, seeing in it at last not merely a tool of black magic, but a sword of good and light against the powers of inhuman evil forever. And he was shaken with a strange reverence for it that was almost fear. Then he bent to the Thing at his feet, shuddering to feel its strange mass slip through his fingers like wisps of heavy fog. He thrust the staff beneath it and somehow lifted and levered the mass back into the mausoleum and shut the door.

Then he stood gazing down at the strangely mutilated body of Hassim, noting how it was smeared with foul slime and how it had already begun to decompose. He shuddered again, and suddenly a low timid voice aroused him from his sombre cogitations. The captives knelt beneath the trees and watched with great patient eyes. With a start he shook off his strange mood. He took from the mouldering corpse his own pistols, dirk and rapier, making shift to wipe off the clinging foulness that was already flecking the steel with rust. He also took up a quantity of powder and shot dropped by the Arabs in their frantic flight. He knew they would return no more. They might die in their flight, or they might gain through the interminable leagues of jungle to the coast; but they would not turn back to dare the terror of that grisly glade.

Kane came to the wretched slaves and after some difficulty released them. "Take up these weapons which the warriors dropped in their haste," said he, "and get you home. This is an evil place. Get ye back to your villages and when the next Arabs come, die in the ruins of your huts rather than be slaves."

Then they would have knelt and kissed his feet but he, in much confusion, forbade them roughly. Then as they made preparations to go, one said to him: "Master, what of thee? Wilt thou not return with us? Thou shalt be our king!"

But Kane shook his head.

"I go eastward," said he. And so the tribespeople bowed to him and turned back on the long trail to their own homeland. And Kane shouldered the staff that had been the rod of the Pharaohs and of Moses and of Solomon and of nameless Atlantean kings behind them, and turned his face eastward, halting only for a single backward glance at the great mausoleum that other Solomon had built with strange arts so long ago, and which now loomed dark and forever silent against the stars.

Wings in the Night *(Robert E. Howard)*

I. — THE HORROR ON THE STAKE

SOLOMON KANE leaned on his strangely carved staff and gazed in scowling perplexity at the mystery which spread silently before him. Many a deserted village Kane had seen in the months that had passed since he turned his face east from the Slave Coast and lost himself in the mazes of jungle and river, but never one like this.

It was not famine that had driven away the inhabitants, for yonder the wild rice still grew rank and unkempt in the untilled fields. There were no Arab slave-raiders in this nameless land— it must have been a tribal war that devastated the village, Kane decided, as he gazed sombrely at the scattered bones and grinning skulls that littered the space among the rank weeds and grasses. These bones were shattered and splintered, and Kane saw jackals and a hyena furtively slinking among the ruined huts. But why had the slayers left the spoils? There lay war spears, their shafts crumbling before the attacks of the white ants. There lay shields, mouldering in the rains and sun. There lay the cooking pots, and about the neck-bones of a shattered skeleton glistened a necklace of gaudily painted pebbles and shells—surely rare loot for any savage conqueror.

He gazed at the huts, wondering why the thatch roofs of so many were torn and rent, as if by taloned things seeking entrance. Then something made his cold eyes narrow in startled unbelief. Just outside the mouldering mound that was once the village wall towered a gigantic baobab tree, branchless for sixty feet, its mighty bole too large to be gripped and scaled. Yet in the topmost branches dangled a skeleton, apparently impaled on a broken limb.

The cold hand of mystery touched the shoulder of Solomon Kane. How came those pitiful remains in that tree? Had some monstrous ogre's inhuman hand flung them there?

Kane shrugged his broad shoulders and his hand unconsciously touched the black butts of his heavy pistols, the hilt of his long rapier, and the dirk in his belt. Kane felt no fear as an ordinary man would feel, confronted with the Unknown and Nameless. Years of wandering in strange lands and warring with strange creatures had melted away from brain, soul, and body all that was not steel and whalebone. He was tall and spare, almost gaunt, built with the savage economy of the wolf. Broad-shouldered, long-armed, with nerves of ice and thews of spring steel, he was no less the natural killer than the born swordsman.

The brambles and thorns of the jungle had dealt hardly with him; his garments hung in tatters, his featherless slouch hat was torn and his boots of Cordovan leather were scratched and worn. The sun had baked his chest and limbs to a deep bronze, but his ascetically lean face was impervious to its rays. His complexion was still of that strange, dark pallor which gave him an almost corpse-like appearance, belied only by his cold, light eyes.

And now Kane, sweeping the village once more with his searching gaze, pulled his belt into a more comfortable position, shifted to his left hand the cat-headed stave N'Longa had given him, and took up his way again.

To the west lay a strip of thin forest, sloping downward to a broad belt of savannas, a waving sea of grass waist-deep and deeper. Beyond that rose another narrow strip of woodlands, deepening rapidly into dense jungle. Out of that jungle Kane had fled like a hunted wolf with pointed-toothed men hot on his trail. Even now a vagrant breeze brought faintly the throb of a savage drum which whispered its obscene tale of hate and blood-hunger and belly-lust across miles of jungle and grassland.

The memory of his flight and narrow escape was vivid in Kane's mind, for only the day before had he realized too late that he was in cannibal country, and all that afternoon in the reeking stench of the thick jungle, he had crept and run and hidden and doubled and twisted on his track with the fierce hunters ever close behind him, until night fell and he gained and crossed the grasslands under cover of darkness.

Now in the late morning he had seen nothing, heard nothing of his pursuers, yet he had no reason to believe that they had abandoned the chase. They had been close on his heels when he took to the savannas.

So Kane surveyed the land in front of him. To the east, curving from north to south ran a straggling range of hills, for the most part dry and barren, rising in the south to a jagged black skyline that reminded Kane of the black hills of Negari. Between him and these hills stretched a broad expanse of gently rolling country, thickly treed, but nowhere approaching the density of a jungle. Kane got the impression of a vast upland plateau, bounded by the curving hills to the east and by the savannas to the west.

Kane set out for the hills with his long, swinging, tireless stride. Surely somewhere behind him the savage demons were stealing after him, and he had no desire to be driven to bay. A shot might send them flying in sudden terror, but on the other hand, so low they were in the scale of humanity, it might transmit no supernatural fear to their dull brains. And not even Solomon Kane, whom Sir Francis Drake had called Devon's king of swords, could win in a pitched battle with a whole tribe.

The silent village with its burden of death and mystery faded out behind him. Utter silence reigned among these mysterious uplands where no birds sang and only a silent macaw flitted among the great trees. The only sounds were Kane's cat-like tread, and the whisper of the drum-haunted breeze.

And then Kane caught a glimpse among the trees that made his heart leap with a sudden, nameless horror, and a few moments later he stood before Horror itself, stark and grisly. In a wide clearing, on a rather bold incline stood a grim stake, and to this stake was bound a thing that had once been a man. Kane had rowed, chained to the bench of a Turkish galley, and he had toiled in Barbary vineyards; he had battled red Indians in the New Lands and had languished in the dungeons of Spain's Inquisition. He knew much of the fiendishness of man's inhumanity, but now he shuddered and grew sick. Yet it was not so much the ghastliness of the mutilations, horrible as they were, that shook Kane's soul, but the knowledge that the wretch still lived.

For as he drew near, the gory head that lolled on the butchered breast lifted and tossed from side to side, spattering blood from the stumps of ears, while a bestial, rattling whimper drooled from the shredded lips.

Kane spoke to the ghastly thing and it screamed unbearably, writhing in incredible contortions, while its head jerked up and down with the jerking of mangled nerves, and the empty, gaping eye-sockets seemed striving to see from their emptiness. And moaning low and brain-shatteringly it huddled its outraged self against the stake where it was bound and lifted its head in a grisly attitude of listening, as if it expected something out of the skies.

"Listen," said Kane, in the dialect of the river tribes. "Do not fear me—I will not harm you and nothing else shall harm you any more. I am going to loose you."

Even as he spoke Kane was bitterly aware of the emptiness of his words. But his voice had filtered dimly into the crumbling, agony-shot brain of the man before him. From between splintered teeth fell words, faltering and uncertain, mixed and mingled with the slavering droolings of imbecility. He spoke a language akin to the dialects Kane had learned from friendly river folk on his wanderings, and Kane gathered that he had been bound to the stake for a long time—many moons, he whimpered in the delirium of approaching death; and all this time, inhuman, evil things had worked their monstrous will upon him. These things he mentioned by name, but Kane could make nothing of it for he used an unfamiliar term that sounded like Akaana. But these things had not bound him to the stake, for the torn wretch slavered the name of Goru, who was a priest and who had drawn a cord too tight about his legs—and Kane wondered that the memory of this small pain should linger through the red mazes of agony that the dying man should whimper over it.

And to Kane's horror, the man spoke of his brother who had aided in the binding of him, and he wept with infantile sobs. Moisture formed in the empty sockets and made tears of blood. And he muttered of a spear broken long ago in some dim hunt, and while he muttered in his delirium, Kane gently cut his bonds and eased his broken body to the grass. But even at the Englishman's careful touch, the poor wretch writhed and howled like a dying dog, while blood started anew from a score of ghastly gashes, which, Kane noted, were more like the wounds made by fang and talon than by knife or spear. But at last it was done and the bloody, torn thing lay on the soft grass with Kane's, old slouch hat beneath its death's-head, breathing in great, rattling gasps.

Kane poured water from his canteen between the mangled lips, and bending close, said: "Tell me more of these devils, for by the God of my people, this deed shall not go unavenged, though Satan himself bar my way."

It is doubtful if the dying man heard. But he heard something else. The macaw, with the curiosity of its breed, swept from a near-by grove and passed so close its great wings fanned Kane's hair. And at the sound of those wings, the butchered man heaved upright and screamed in a voice that haunted Kane's dreams to the day of his death: "The wings! the wings! They come again! Ahhh, mercy, the wings!"

And the blood burst in a torrent from his lips and so he died.

Kane rose and wiped the cold sweat from his forehead. The upland forest shimmered in the noonday heat. Silence lay over the land like an enchantment of dreams. Kane's brooding eyes ranged to the black, malevolent hills crouching in the distance and back to the far-away savannas. An ancient curse lay over that mysterious land and the shadow of it fell across the soul of Solomon Kane.

Tenderly he lifted the red ruin that had once pulsed with life and youth and vitality, and carried it to the edge of the glade, where arranging the cold limbs as best he might, and shuddering once again at the unnameable mutilations, he piled stones above it till even a prowling jackal would find it hard to get at the flesh below.

And he had scarcely finished when something jerked him back out of his sombre broodings to a realization of his own position. A slight sound—or his own wolf-like instinct—made him whirl.

On the other side of the glade he caught a movement among the tall grasses—the glimpse of a hideous face, with an ivory ring in the flat nose, thick lips parted to reveal teeth whose filed points were apparent even at that distance, beady eyes and a low slanting forehead topped by a mop of frizzy hair. Even as the face faded from view Kane leaped back into the shelter of the ring of trees which circled the glade, and ran like a deer-hound, flitting from tree to tree and expecting at each moment to hear the exultant clamour of the warriors and to see them break cover at his back.

But soon he decided that they were content to hunt him down as certain beasts track their prey, slowly and inevitably. He hastened through the upland forest, taking advantage of every bit of cover, and he saw no more of his pursuers; yet he knew, as a hunted wolf knows, that they hovered close behind him, waiting their moment to strike him down without risk to their own hides.

Kane smiled bleakly and without mirth, If it was to be a test of endurance, he would see how savage thews compared with his own spring-steel resilience. Let night come and he might yet give them the slip. If not—Kane knew in his heart that the savage essence of his very being which chafed at his flight, would make him soon turn at bay, though his pursuers outnumbered him a hundred to one.

The sun sank westward. Kane was hungry, for he had not eaten since early morning when he wolfed down the last of his dried meat. An occasional spring had given him water, and once he thought he glimpsed the roof of a large hut far away through the trees. But he gave it a wide berth. It was hard to believe that this silent plateau was inhabited, but if it were, the natives were doubtless as ferocious as those hunting him.

Ahead of him the land grew rougher, with broken boulders and steep slopes as he neared the lower reaches of the brooding hills. And still no sight of his hunters except for faint glimpses caught by wary backward glances—a drifting shadow, the bending of the grass, the sudden straightening of a trodden twig, a rustle of leaves. Why should they be so cautious? Why did they not close in and have it over?

Night fell and Kane reached the first long slopes which led upward to the foot of the hills which now brooded black and menacing above him. They were his goal, where he hoped to shake off his persistent foes at last, yet a nameless aversion warned him away from them. They were pregnant with hidden evil, repellent as the coil of a great sleeping serpent, glimpsed in the tall grass.

Darkness fell heavily. The stars winked redly in the thick heat of the tropic night. And Kane, halting for a moment in an unusually dense grove, beyond which the trees thinned out on the slopes, heard a stealthy movement that was not the night wind—for no breath of air stirred the heavy leaves. And even as he turned, there was a rush in the dark, under the trees.

A shadow that merged with the shadows flung itself on Kane with a bestial mouthing and a rattle of iron, and the Englishman, parrying by the gleam of the stars on the weapon, felt his assailant duck into close quarters and meet him chest to chest. Lean wiry arms locked about him, pointed teeth gnashed at him as Kane returned the fierce grapple. His tattered shirt ripped beneath a jagged edge, and by blind chance Kane found and pinioned the hand that held the iron knife, and drew his own dirk, flesh crawling in anticipation of a spear in the back.

But even as the Englishman wondered why the others did not come to their comrade's aid, he threw all of his iron muscles into the single combat. Close-clinched they swayed and writhed in the darkness, each striving to drive his blade into the other's flesh, and as the superior strength of the Puritan began to assert itself, the cannibal howled like a rabid dog, tore and bit.

A convulsive spin-wheel of effort pivoted them out into the starlit glade where Kane saw the ivory nose-ring and the pointed teeth that snapped beast-like at his throat. And simultaneously he forced back and down the hand that gripped his knife-wrist, and drove the dirk deep into the savage wrists. The warrior screamed, and the raw acrid scent of blood flooded the night air. And in that instant Kane was stunned by a sudden savage rush and beat of mighty wings that dashed him to earth, and the cannibal was torn from his grip and vanished with a scream of mortal agony. Kane leaped to his feet, shaken to his foundation. The dwindling scream of the wretched savage sounded faintly and from above him.

Straining his eyes into the skies he thought he caught a glimpse of a shapeless and horrific Thing crossing the dim stars—in which the writhing limbs of a human mingled namelessly with great wings and a shadowy shape—but so quickly it was gone, he could not be sure.

And now he wondered if it were not all a nightmare. But groping in the grove he found the ju-ju stave with which he had parried the short stabbing spear that lay beside it. And here, if more proof was needed, was his long dirk, still stained with blood.

Wings! Wings in the night! The skeleton in the village of torn roofs—the mutilated warrior whose wounds were not made with knife or spear and who died shrieking of wings. Surely those hills were the haunt of gigantic birds who made humanity their prey. Yet if birds, why had they not wholly devoured the torn man on the stake? And Kane knew in his heart that no true bird ever cast such a shadow as he had seen flit across the stars.

He shrugged his shoulders, bewildered. The night was silent. Where were the rest of the cannibals who had followed him from their distant jungle? Had the fate of their comrade frightened them into flight? Kane looked to his pistols. Cannibals or no, he went not up into those dark hills that night.

Now he must sleep, if all the devils of the Elder World were on his track. A deep roaring to the westward warned him that beasts of prey were aroam, and he walked rapidly down the rolling slopes until he came to a dense grove some distance from that in which he had fought the cannibal. He climbed high among the great branches until he found a thick crotch that would accommodate even his tall frame. The branches above would guard him from a sudden swoop of any winged thing, and if savages were lurking near, their clamber into the tree would warn him, for he slept lightly as a cat. As for serpents and leopards, they were chances he had taken a thousand times.

Solomon Kane slept and his dreams were vague, chaotic, haunted with a suggestion of pre-human evil and which at last merged into a vision vivid as a scene in waking life. Solomon dreamed he woke with a start, drawing a pistol—for so long had his life been that of the wolf, that reaching for a weapon was his natural reaction upon waking suddenly.

His dream was that a strange, shadowy thing had perched upon a great branch close by and gazed at him with greedy, luminous yellow eyes that seared into his brain. The dream-thing was tall and lean and strangely misshapen, so blended with the shadows that it seemed a shadow itself, tangible only in the narrow yellow eyes. And Kane dreamed he waited, spellbound, while uncertainty came into those eyes, and then the creature walked out on the limb as a man would walk, raised great shadowy wings, sprang into space and vanished.

Kane jerked upright, the mists of sleep fading. In the dim starlight, under the arching Gothic-like branches, the tree was empty save for himself. Then it had been a dream, after all—yet it had been so vivid, so fraught with inhuman foulness—even now a faint scent like that exuded by birds of prey seemed to linger in the air. Kane strained his ears. He heard the sighing of the night wind, the whisper of the leaves, the far-away roaring of a lion, but naught else. Again Solomon slept—while high above him a shadow wheeled against the stars, circling again and again as a vulture circles a dying wolf.

II. — THE BATTLE IN THE SKY

DAWN was spreading whitely over the eastern hills when Kane woke. The thought of his nightmare came to him and he wondered again at its vividness as he climbed down out of the tree. A nearby spring slaked his thirst and some fruit, rare in these highlands, eased his hunger.

Then he turned his face again to the hills. A finish fighter was Solomon Kane. Along that grim skyline dwelt some evil foe to the sons of men, and that mere fact was as much a challenge to the Puritan as had ever been a glove thrown in his face by some hot-headed gallant of Devon.

Refreshed by his night's sleep, he set out with his long easy stride, passing the grove that had witnessed the battle in the night, and coming into the region where the trees thinned at the foot of the slopes. Up these slopes he went, halting for a moment to gaze back over the way he had come. Now that he was above

the plateau, he could easily make out a village in the distance —
a cluster of mud-and-bamboo huts with one unusually large hut
a short distance from the rest on a sort of low knoll.

And while he gazed, with a sudden rush of grisly wings the
terror was upon him! Kane whirled, galvanized. All signs had
pointed to the theory of a winged thing that hunted by night. He
had not expected attack in broad daylight—but here a bat-like
monster was swooping at him out of the very eye of the rising
sun. Kane saw a spread of mighty wings, from which glared a
horribly human face; then he drew and fired with unerring aim
and the monster veered wildly in midair and came whirling and
tumbling out of the sky to crash at his feet.

Kane leaned forward, pistol smoking in his hand, and gazed
wide-eyed. Surely this thing was a demon out of the pits of hell,
said the sombre mind of the Puritan; yet a leaden ball had slain
it. Kane shrugged his shoulders, baffled; he had never seen
aught to approach this, though all his life had fallen in strange
ways.

The thing was like a man, inhumanly tall and inhumanly thin;
the head was long, narrow, and hairless—the head of a predatory
creature. The ears were small, close-set and queerly pointed. The
eyes, set in death, were narrow, oblique and of a strange
yellowish colour. The nose was thin and hooked, like the beak of
a bird of prey, the mouth a wide cruel gash, whose thin lips,
writhed in a death snarl and flecked with foam, disclosed wolfish
fangs.

The creature, which was naked and hairless, was not unlike a
human being in other ways. The shoulders were broad and
powerful, the neck long and lean. The arms were long and
muscular, the thumb being set beside the fingers after the
manner of the great apes. Fingers and thumbs were armed with
heavy hooked talons. The chest was curiously misshapen, the
breast-bone jutting out like the keel of a ship, the ribs curving
back from it. The legs were long and wiry with huge, hand-like,

prehensile feet, the great toe set opposite the rest like a man's thumb. The claws on the toes were merely long nails.

But the most curious feature of this curious creature was on its back. A pair of great wings, shaped much like the wings of a moth but with a bony frame and of leathery substance, grew from its shoulders, beginning at a point just back and above where the arms joined the shoulders, and extending half way to the narrow hips. These wings, Kane reckoned, would measure some eighteen feet from tip to tip.

He laid hold of the creature, involuntarily shuddering at the slick, hard, leather-like feel of the skin, and half-lifted it. The weight was little more than half as much as it would have been in a man the same height—some six and a half feet. Evidently the bones were of a peculiar bird-like structure and the flesh consisted almost entirely of stringy muscles.

Kane stepped back, surveying the thing again. Then his dream had been no dream after all—that foul thing or another like it had in grisly reality lighted in the tree beside him—a whir of mighty wings! A sudden rush through the sky! Even as Kane whirled he realized he had committed the jungle-farer's unpardonable crime—he had allowed his astonishment and curiosity to throw him off guard. Already a winged fiend was at his throat and there was no time to draw and fire his other pistol. Kane saw, in a maze of thrashing wings, a devilish, semi-human face—he felt those wings battering at him—he felt cruel talons sink deep into his breast; then he was dragged off his feet and felt empty space beneath him.

The winged man had wrapped his limbs about the Englishman's legs and the talons he had driven into Kane's breast muscles held like fanged vices. The wolf-like fangs drove at Kane's throat, but the Puritan gripped the bony throat and thrust back the grisly head, while with his right hand he strove to draw his dirk. The birdman was mounting slowly and a fleeting glance showed Kane that they were already high above the trees. The Englishman did not hope to survive this battle in the sky, for even if he slew his foe, he would be dashed to death in the fall. But with the innate ferocity of the fighting man he set himself grimly to take his captor with him.

Holding those keen fangs at bay, Kane managed to draw his dirk, and he plunged it deep into the body of the monster. The bat-man veered wildly and a rasping, raucous screech burst from his half-throttled throat. He floundered wildly, beating frantically with his great wings, bowing his back and twisting his head fiercely in a vain effort to free it and sink home his deadly fangs. He sank the talons of one hand agonizingly deeper and deeper into Kane's breast muscles, while with the other he tore at his foe's head and body. But the Englishman, gashed and bleeding, with the silent and tenacious savagery of a bulldog, sank his fingers deeper into the lean neck and drove his dirk home again and again, while far below awed eyes watched the fiendish battle that was raging at that dizzy height.

They had drifted out over the plateau, and the fast-weakening wings of the bat-man barely supported their weight. They were sinking earthward swiftly, but Kane, blinded with blood and battle fury, knew nothing of this. With a great piece of his scalp hanging loose, his chest and shoulders cut and ripped, the world had become a blind, red thing in which he was aware of but one sensation—the bulldog urge to kill his foe.

Now the feeble and spasmodic beating of the dying monster's wings held them hovering for an instant above a thick grove of gigantic trees, while Kane felt the grip of claws and twining limbs grow weaker and the slashing of the talons become a futile flailing.

With a last burst of power he drove the reddened dirk straight through the breastbone and felt a convulsive tremor run through the creature's frame. The great wings fell limp—and victor and vanquished dropped headlong and plummet-like earthward.

Through a red wave Kane saw the waving branches rushing up to meet them—he felt them flail his face and tear at his clothing, as still locked in that death-clinch he rushed downward through

leaves which eluded his vainly grasping hand; then his head
crashed against a great limb, and an endless abyss of blackness
engulfed him.

III. — THE PEOPLE IN THE SHADOW

THROUGH colossal, black basaltic corridors of night, Solomon
Kane fled for a thousand years. Gigantic winged demons, horrific
in the utter darkness, swept over him with a rush of great bat-
like pinions and in the blackness he fought with them as a
cornered rat fights a vampire bat, while fleshless jaws drooled
fearful blasphemies and horrid secrets in his ears, and the skulls
of men rolled under his groping feet.

Solomon Kane came back suddenly from the land of delirium,
and his first sight of sanity was that of a fat, kindly native face
bending over him. Kane saw he was in a roomy, clean and well-
ventilated hut, while from a cooking pot bubbling outside wafted
savoury scents. Kane realized he was ravenously hungry. And he
was strangely weak. The hand he lifted to his bandaged head
shook, and its bronze was dimmed.

The fat man and another, a tall, gaunt, grim-faced warrior, bent
over him, and the fat man said: "He is awake, Kuroba, and of
sound mind." The gaunt man nodded and called something which
was answered from without.

"What is this place?" asked Kane in a language he had learned
that was similar to the dialect just used. "How long have I lain
here?"

"This is the last village of Bogonda." The fat man pressed him
back with hands as gentle as a woman's. "We found you lying
beneath the trees on the slopes, badly wounded and senseless.
You have raved in delirium for many days. Now eat."

A lithe young warrior entered with a wooden bowl full of
steaming food, and Kane ate ravenously. "He is like a leopard,

Kuroba," said the fat man admiringly. "Not one in a thousand would have lived with his wounds."

"Aye," returned the other. "And he slew the akaana that rent him, Goru."

Kane struggled to his elbows. "Goru?" he cried fiercely. "The priest who binds men to stakes for devils to eat?"

And he strove to rise so that he could strangle the fat man, but his weakness swept over him like a wave, the hut swam dizzily to his eyes, and he sank back panting, where he soon fell into a sound, natural sleep.

Later he awoke and found a slim young girl, named Nayela, watching him. She fed him, and feeling much stronger, Kane asked questions which she answered shyly but intelligently.

This was Bogonda, ruled by Kuroba the chief and Goru the priest. None in Bogonda had ever seen or heard of a white man before. She counted the days Kane had lain helpless, and he was amazed. But such a battle as he had been through was enough to kill an ordinary man. He wondered that no bones had been broken, but the girl said the branches had broken his fall and he had landed on the body of the akaana. He asked for Goru, and the fat priest came to him, bringing Kane's weapons.

"Some we found with you where you lay." said Goru, "some by the body of the akaana you slew with the weapon which speaks in fire and smoke. You must be a god—yet the gods bleed not and you have just all but died. Who are you?"

"I am no god," Kane answered, "but a man like yourself. I come from a far land amid the sea, which land, mind ye, is the fairest and noblest of all lands. My name is Solomon Kane and I am a landless wanderer. From the lips of a dying man I first heard your name. Yet your face seemeth kindly."

A shadow crossed the eyes of the shaman, and he hung his head.

"Rest and grow strong, oh man, or god or whatever you be," said he, "and in time you will learn of the ancient curse that rests upon this ancient land."

And in the days that followed, while Kane recovered and grew strong with the wild beast vitality that was his, Goru and Kuroba sat and spoke to him at length, telling him many curious things.

Their tribe was not aboriginal here, but had come upon the plateau a hundred and fifty years before, giving it the name of their former home. They had once been a powerful tribe in Old Bogonda, on a great river far to the south. But tribal wars broke their power, and at last before a concerted uprising, the whole tribe gave way, and Goru repeated legends of that great flight of a thousand miles through jungle and swampland, harried at every step by cruel foes.

At last, hacking their way through a country of ferocious cannibals, they found themselves safe from man's attack—but prisoners in a trap from which neither they nor their descendants could ever escape. They were in the horror-country of Akaana, and Goru said his ancestors came to understand the jeering laughter of the man eaters who had hounded them to the very borders of the plateau.

The Bogondi found a fertile country with good water and plenty of game. There were numbers of goats and a species of wild pig that throve here in great abundance. At first the people ate these pigs, but later they spared them for a good reason. The grasslands between plateau and jungle swarmed with antelopes, buffaloes and the like, and there were many lions. Lions also roamed the plateau, but Bogonda meant "Lion-slayer" in their tongue and it was not many moons before the remnants of the great cats took to the lower levels. But it was not lions they had to fear, as Goru's ancestors soon learned.

Finding that the cannibals would not come past the savannas, they rested from their long trek and built two villages—Upper and Lower Bogonda. Kane was in Upper Bogonda; he had seen the ruins of the lower village. But soon they found that they had strayed into a country of nightmares with dripping fangs and talons. They heard the beat of mighty wings at night, and saw horrific shadows cross the stars and loom against the moon. Children began to disappear and at last a young hunter strayed off into the hills, where night overtook him. And in the grey light of dawn a mangled, half-devoured corpse fell from the skies into the village street and a whisper of ogreish laughter from high above froze the horrified on-lookers. Then a little later the full horror of their position burst upon the Bogondi.

At first the winged men were afraid of the newcomers. They hid themselves and ventured from their caverns only at night. Then they grew bolder. In the full daylight, a warrior shot one with an arrow, but the fiends had learned they could slay a human, and its death scream brought a score of the devils dropping from the skies, who tore the slayer to pieces in full sight of the tribe.

The Bogondi then prepared to leave that devil's country and a hundred warriors went up into the hills to find a pass. They found steep walls, up which a man must climb laboriously, and they found the cliffs honeycombed with caves where the winged men dwelt.

Then was fought the first pitched battle between men and bat-men, and it resulted in a crushing victory for the monsters. The bows and spears of the natives proved futile before the swoops of the taloned fiends, and of all that hundred that went up into the hills, not one survived; for the akaanas hunted down those that fled and dragged down the last one within bowshot of the upper village.

Then it was that the Bogondi, seeing they could not hope to win through the hills, sought to fight their way out again the way they had come. But a great horde of cannibals met them in the grasslands, and in a great battle that lasted nearly all day, hurled them back, broken and defeated. And Goru said while the battle raged, the skies were thronged with hideous shapes, circling above and laughing their fearful mirth to see men die wholesale.

So the survivors of those two battles, licking their wounds, bowed to the inevitable with the fatalistic philosophy of the savage. Some fifteen hundred men, women and children remained, and they built their huts, tilled the soil and lived stolidly in the shadow of the nightmare.

In those days there were many of the bird-people, and they might have wiped out the Bogondi utterly, had they wished. No one warrior could cope with an akaana, for he was stronger than a human, he struck as a hawk strikes, and if he missed, his wings carried him out of reach of a counterblow.

Here Kane interrupted to ask why the Bogondi did not make war on the demons with arrows. But Goru answered that it took a quick and accurate archer to strike an akaana in midair at all, and so tough were their hides that unless the arrow struck squarely it would not penetrate. Kane knew that the natives were very indifferent bowmen and that they pointed their shafts with chipped stone, bone, or hammered iron almost as soft as copper; he thought of Poitiers and Agincourt and wished grimly for a file of stout English archers—or a rank of musketeers.

But Goru said the akaanas did not seem to wish to destroy the Bogondi utterly. Their chief food consisted of the little pigs which then swarmed the plateau, and young goats. Sometimes they went out on the savannas for antelope, but they distrusted the open country and feared the lions. Nor did they haunt the jungles beyond, for the trees grew too close for the spread of their wings. They kept to the hills and the plateau—and what lay beyond those hills none in Bogonda knew.

The akaanas allowed the Bogondi to inhabit the plateau much as men allow wild animals to thrive, or stock lakes with fish—for their own pleasure. The bat-people, said Goru, had a strange and grisly sense of humour which was tickled by the sufferings of a howling human. Those grim hills had echoed to cries that turned men's hearts to ice.

But for many years, Goru said, once the Bogondi learned not to resist their masters, the akaanas were content to snatch up a baby from time to time, or devour a young girl strayed from the village or a youth whom night caught outside the walls. The bat-folk distrusted the village; they circled high above it but did not venture within. There the Bogondi were safe until late years.

Goru said that the akaanas were fast dying out; once there had been hope that the remnants of his race would outlast them—in which event, he said fatalistically, the cannibals would undoubtedly come up from the jungle and put the survivors in their cooking pots. Now he doubted if there were more than a hundred and fifty akaanas altogether. Kane asked him why did not the warriors then sally forth on a great hunt and destroy the devils utterly, and Goru smiled a bitter smile and repeated his remarks about the prowess of the bat-people in battle. Moreover, said he, the whole tribe of Bogonda numbered only about four hundred souls now, and the bat-people were their only protection against the cannibals to the west.

Goru said the tribe had thinned more in the past thirty years than in all the years previous. As the numbers of the akaanas dwindled, their hellish savagery increased. They seized more and more of the Bogondi to torture and devour in their grim black caves high up in the hills, and Goru spoke of sudden raids on hunting parties and toilers in the plantain fields, and of the nights made ghastly by horrible screams and gibberings from the dark hills, and blood-freezing laughter that was half-human; of dismembered limbs and gory grinning heads flung from the skies to fall in the shuddering village, and of grisly feasts among the stars.

Then came drought, Goru said, and a great famine. Many of the springs dried up and the crops of rice and yams and plantains failed. The gnus, deer, and buffaloes which had formed the main part of Bogonda's meat diet withdrew to the jungle in quest of water, and the lions, their hunger overcoming their fear of man, ranged into the uplands. Many of the tribe died, and the rest were driven by hunger to eat the pigs which were the natural prey of the bat-people. This angered the akaanas and thinned the pigs. Famine, Bogondi, and the lions destroyed all the goats and half the pigs.

At last the famine was past, but the damage was done. Of all the great droves which once swarmed the plateau, only a remnant was left, and these were hard to catch. The Bogondi had eaten the pigs, so the akaanas ate the Bogondi. Life became a hell for the humans, and the lower village, numbering now only some hundred and fifty souls, rose in revolt. Driven to frenzy by repeated outrages, they turned on their masters. An akaana lighting in the very streets to steal a child was set on and shot to death with arrows. And the people of Lower Bogonda drew into their huts and waited for their doom.

And in the night, said Goru, it came. The akaanas had overcome their distrust of the huts. The full flock of them swarmed down from the hills, and Upper Bogonda awoke to hear the fearful cataclysm of screams and blasphemies that marked the end of the other village. All night Goru's people had lain sweating in terror, not daring to move, harkening to the howling and gibbering that rent the night. At last these sounds ceased, Goru said, wiping the cold sweat from his brow, but sounds of grisly and obscene feasting still haunted the night with demon's mockery. In the early dawn, Goru's people saw the hell-flock winging back to their hills, like demons flying back to hell through the dawn. They flew slowly and heavily, like gorged vultures. Later the people dared to steal down to the accursed village, and what they found there sent them shrieking away. And to that day, Goru said, no man passed within three bow shots of that silent horror. And Kane nodded in understanding, his cold eyes more sombre man ever.

For many days after that, Goru said the people waited in quaking fear. Finally in desperation of fear, which breeds unspeakable cruelty, the tribe cast lots, and the loser was bound to a stake between the two villages, in hopes that the akaanas would recognize this as a token of submission so that the people of Bogonda might escape the fate of their kinsmen. The custom, said Goru, had been borrowed from the cannibals who in old times worshipped the akaanas and offered a human sacrifice at each moon. But chance had shown them that the akaanas could be killed, so they ceased to worship them—at least that was Goru's deduction, and he explained at much length that no mortal thing is worthy of real adoration, however evil or powerful it may be.

His own ancestors had made occasional sacrifices to placate the winged devils, but until lately it had not been a regular custom. Now it was necessary; the akaanas expected it, and each moon they chose from their waning numbers a strong young man or a girl whom they bound to the stake.

Kane watched Goru's face closely as he spoke of his sorrow for this unspeakable necessity, and the Englishman realized that the priest was sincere. Kane shuddered at the thought of a tribe of human beings thus passing slowly but surely into the maws of a race of monsters.

Kane spoke of the wretch he had seen, and Goru nodded, pain in his soft eyes. For a day and a night he had been hanging there, while the akaanas glutted their vile torture-lust on his quivering, agonized flesh. Thus far the sacrifices had kept doom from the village. The remaining pigs furnished sustenance for the dwindling akaanas, together with an occasional baby snatched up, and they were content to have their nameless sport with the single victim each moon.

A thought came to Kane. "The cannibals never come up into the plateau?" Goru shook his head; safe in their jungle, they never raided past the savannas.

"But they hunted me to the very foot of the hills."

Again Goru shook his head. There was only one cannibal; they had found his footprints. Evidently a single warrior, bolder than the rest, had allowed his passion for the chase to overcome his fear of the grisly plateau and had paid the penalty. Kane's teeth came together with a vicious snap which ordinarily took the place of profanity with him. He was stung by the thought of fleeing so long from a single enemy. No wonder that enemy had followed so cautiously, waiting until dark to attack. But, asked Kane, why had the akaana seized the cannibal instead of himself—and why had he not been attacked by the bat-man who alighted in his tree that night?

The cannibal was bleeding, Goru answered. The scent called the bat-fiend to attack, for they scented raw blood as far as vultures. And they were very wary. They had never seen a man like Kane, who showed no fear. Surely they had decided to spy on him, take him off guard before they struck.

Who were these creatures? Kane asked. Goru shrugged his shoulders. They were there when his ancestors came, who had never heard of them before they saw them. There was no intercourse with the cannibals, so they could learn nothing from them. The akaanas lived in caves, naked like beasts; they knew nothing of fire and ate only fresh, raw meat. But they had a language of a sort and acknowledged a king among them. Many died in the great famine when the stronger ate the weaker. They were vanishing swiftly; of late years no females or young had been observed among them. When these males died at last, there would be no more akaanas; but Bogonda, observed Goru, was doomed already, unless—he looked strangely and wistfully at Kane. But the Puritan was deep in thought.

Among the swarm of native legends he had heard on his wanderings, one now stood out. Long, long ago, an old, old ju-ju man had told him, winged devils came flying out of the north and passed over his country, vanishing in the maze of the jungle-haunted south. And the ju-ju man related an old, old legend concerning these creatures—that once they had abode in myriad numbers far on a great lake of bitter water many moons to the north, and ages and ages ago a chieftain and his warriors fought them with bows and arrows and slew many, driving the rest into the south. The name of the chief was N'Yasunna and he owned a great war canoe with many oars driving it swiftly through the bitter water.

And now a cold wind blew suddenly on Solomon Kane, as if from a door opened suddenly on Outer gulfs of Time and Space. For now he realized the truth of that garbled myth, and the truth of an older, grimmer legend. For what was the great bitter lake but the Mediterranean Ocean and who was the chief N'Yasunna but the hero Jason, who conquered the harpies and drove them—not alone into the Strophades Isles but into Africa as well?

The old pagan tale was true then, Kane thought dizzily, shrinking aghast from the strange realm of grisly possibilities this opened up. For if this myth of the harpies were a reality, what of the other legends—the Hydra, the centaurs, the chimera, Medusa, Pan, and the satyrs?

All those myths of antiquity—behind them did there lie and lurk nightmare realities with slavering fangs and talons steeped in shuddersome evil? Africa, the Dark Continent, land of shadows and horror, of bewitchment and sorcery, into which all evil things had been banished before the growing light of the western world!

Kane came out of his reveries with a start. Goru was tugging gently and timidly at his sleeve.

"Save us from the akaanas!" said Goru. "If you be not a god, there is the power of a god in you! You bear in your hand the mighty ju-ju stave which has in times gone by been the sceptre of fallen empires and the staff of mighty priests. And you have weapons which speak death in fire and smoke—for our young men watched and saw you slay two akaanas. We will make you king —god—what you will! More than a moon has passed since you came into Bogonda and the time for the sacrifice is gone by, but the bloody stake stands bare. The akaanas shun the village where you lie; they steal no more babes from us. We have thrown off their yoke because our trust is in you!"

Kane clasped his temples with his hands. "You know not what you ask!" he cried. "God knoweth it is in my deepest heart to rid the land of this evil, but I am no god. With my pistols I can slay a few of the fiends, but I have but a little powder left. Had I great store of powder and ball, and the musket I shattered in the vampire-haunted Hills of the Dead, then indeed would there be a rare hunting. But even if I slew all those fiends, what of the cannibals?"

"They too will fear you!" cried old Kuroba, while the girl Nayela and the lad, Loga, who was to have been the next sacrifice, gazed at his wife, their souls in their eyes. Kane dropped his chin on his fist and sighed.

"Yet will I stay here in Bogonda all the rest of my life if ye think I be protection to the people."

So Solomon Kane stayed at the village of Bogonda of the Shadow. The people were a kindly folk, whose natural sprightliness and fun-loving spirits were subdued and saddened by long dwelling in the Shadow. But now they had taken new heart by the Englishman's coming, and it wrenched Kane's heart to note the pathetic trust they placed in him. Now they sang in the plaintain fields and danced about the fire, and gazed at him with adoring faith in their eyes. But Kane, cursing his own helplessness, knew how futile would be his fancied protection if the winged fiends swept suddenly out of the skies.

But he stayed in Bogonda. In his dreams, the gulls wheeled above the cliffs of old Devon, carved in the clean, blue, wind-whipped skies, and in the day the call of the unknown lands beyond Bogonda clawed at his heart with fierce yearning. But he abode in Bogonda and racked his brains for a plan. He sat and gazed for hours at the ju-ju stave, hoping in desperation that black magic would aid him, where his mind failed. But N'Longa's ancient gift gave him no aid. Once he had summoned the Slave Coast shaman to him across leagues of intervening space—but it was only when confronted with supernatural manifestations that N'Longa could come to him, and these harpies were not supernatural.

The germ of an idea began to grow at the back of Kane's mind, but he discarded it. It had to do with a great trap—and how could the akaanas be trapped? The roaring of lions played a grim accompaniment to his brooding meditations. As man dwindled on the plateau, the hunting beasts who feared only the spears of the hunters were beginning to gather. Kane laughed bitterly. It was not lions, that might be hunted down and slain singly, that he had to deal with.

At some little distance from the village stood the great hut of Goru, once a council hall. This hut was full of many strange fetishes which, Goru said with a helpless wave of his fat hands, were strong magic against evil spirits but scant protection against winged hellions of gristle and bone and flesh.

IV. — THE MADNESS OF SOLOMON

KANE woke suddenly from a dreamless sleep. A hideous medley of screams burst horrific in his ears. Outside his hut, people were dying in the night, horribly, as cattle die in the shambles. He had slept, as always, with his weapons buckled on him. Now he bounded to the door, and something fell mouthing and slavering at his feet to grasp his knees in a convulsive grin and gibber incoherent pleas.

In the faint light of a smouldering fire near by, Kane in horror recognized the face of the youth Loga, now frightfully torn and drenched in blood, already freezing into a death mask. The night was full of fearful sounds, inhuman howling mingled with the whisper of mighty wings, the tearing of thatch and a ghastly demon-laughter. Kane freed himself from the locked dead arms and sprang to the dying fire. He could make out only a confused and vague maze of fleeing forms and darting shapes, the shift and blur of dark wings against the stars.

He snatched up a brand and thrust it against the thatch of his hut—and as the flame leaped up and showed him the scene he stood frozen and aghast. Red, howling doom had fallen on Bogonda. Winged monsters raced screaming through her streets, wheeled above the heads of the fleeing people, or tore apart the hut thatches to get at the gibbering victims within.

With a choked cry the Englishman woke from his trance of horror, drew and fired at a darting flame-eyed shadow which fell at his feet with a shattered skull. And Kane gave tongue to one deep, fierce roar and bounded into the melee, all the berserk fury of his heathen Saxon ancestors bursting into terrible being.

Dazed and bewildered by the sudden attack, cowed by long years of submission, the Bogondi were incapable of combined resistance and for the most part died like sheep. Some, maddened by desperation, fought back, but their arrows went wild or glanced from the tough wings while the devilish agility of the creatures made spear thrust and axe stroke uncertain. Leaping from the ground they avoided the blows of their victims and, sweeping down upon their shoulders, dashed them to earth where fang and talon did their crimson work.

Kane saw old Kuroba, gaunt and bloodstained, at bay against a hut wall with his foot on the neck of a monster who had not been quick enough. The grim-faced old chief wielded a two-handed axe in great sweeping blows that for the moment held back the screeching onset of half a dozen of the devils. Kane was leaping to his aid when a low, pitiful whimper checked him. The girl Nayela writhed weakly, prone in the bloody dust, while on her back a vulture-like thing crouched and tore. Her dulling eyes sought the face of the Englishman in anguished appeal.

Kane ripped out a bitter oath and fired point blank. The winged devil pitched backward with an abhorrent screeching and a wild flutter of dying wings, and Kane bent to the dying girl. She whimpered and kissed his hands with uncertain lips as he cradled her head in his arms. Her eyes set.

Kane laid the body gently down, looking for Kuroba. He saw only a huddled cluster of grisly shapes that sucked and tore at something between them. And Kane went mad. With a scream that cut through the inferno he bounded up, slaying even as he rose. Even in the act of lunging up from bent knee he drew and thrust, transfixing a vulture-like throat. Then whipping out his rapier as the thing floundered and twitched in its death struggle, the raging Puritan charged forward seeking new victims.

On all sides of him the people of Bogonda were dying hideously. They fought futilely or they fled and the demons coursed them down as a hawk courses a hare. They ran into the huts and the fiends rent the thatch or burst the door, and what took place in those huts was mercifully hidden from Kane's eyes.

And to the frantic Puritan's horror-distorted brain it seemed that he alone was responsible. The Bogondi had trusted him to save them. They had withheld the sacrifice and defied their grim masters. Now they were paying the horrible penalty and he was unable to save them. In the agony-dimmed eyes turned toward him, Kane quaffed the black dregs of the bitter cup. It was hot anger or the vindictiveness of fear. It was hurt and a stunned reproach. He was their god and he had failed them.

Now he ravened through the massacre and the fiends avoided him, turning to the easy victims. But Kane was not to be denied. In a red haze that was not of the burning hut, he saw a culminating horror; a harpy gripped a writhing naked thing that had been a woman, and the wolfish fangs gorged deep. As Kane sprang, thrusting, the bat-man dropped his yammering, mewing prey and soared aloft. But Kane dropped his rapier and with the bound of a blood-mad panther caught the demon's throat and locked his iron legs about its lower body.

Once again he found himself battling in mid-air, but this time close above the hut roofs. Terror had entered the cold brain of the harpy. He did not fight to hold and slay; he wished only to be rid of this silent, clinging thing that stabbed so savagely for his life. He floundered wildly, screaming abhorrently and thrashing with his wings, then as Kane's dirk bit deeper, dipped suddenly sidewise and fell headlong.

The thatch of a hut broke their fall, and Kane and the dying harpy crashed through to land on a writhing mass on the hut floor. In the lurid flickering of the burning hut outside that vaguely lighted the hut into which he had fallen, Kane saw a deed of brain-shaking horror being enacted—red-dripping fangs in a yawning gash of a mouth, and a crimson travesty of a human form that still writhed with agonized life. Then, in the maze of madness that held him, his steel fingers closed on the fiend's throat in a grip that no tearing of talons or hammering of wings could loosen, until he felt the horrid life flow out from under his fingers and the bony neck hung broken.

Outside, the red madness of slaughter continued. Kane bounded up, his hand closing blindly on the haft of some weapon, and as he leaped from the hut a harpy soared from under his very feet. It was an axe that Kane had snatched up, and he dealt a stroke that spattered the demon's brains like water. He sprang forward, stumbling over bodies and parts of bodies, blood streaming from a dozen wounds, and then halted baffled and screaming with rage.

The bat-people were taking to the air. No longer would they face this strange madman who in his insanity was more terrible than they. But they went not alone into the upper regions. In their lustful talons they bore writhing, screaming forms, and Kane, raging to and fro with his dripping axe, found himself alone in a corpse-choked village.

He threw back his head to shriek his hate at the fiends above him and he felt warm, thick drops fall into his face, while the shadowy skies were filled with screams of agony and the laughter of monsters.

As the sounds of that ghastly feast in the skies filled the night and the blood that rained from the stars fell into his face, Kane's last vestige of reason snapped. He gibbered to and fro, screaming chaotic blasphemies.

And was he not a symbol of Man, staggering among the tooth-marked bones and severed grinning heads of humans, brandishing a futile axe, and screaming incoherent hate at the grisly, winged shapes of Night that make him their prey, chuckling in demoniac triumph above him and dripping into his mad eyes the pitiful blood of their human victims?

V. — THE CONQUEROR

A SHUDDERING, white-faced dawn crept over the black hills to shiver above the red shambles that had been the village of Bogonda. The huts stood intact, except for the one which had sunk to smouldering coals, but the thatches of many were torn. Dismembered bones, half or wholly stripped of flesh, lay in the streets, and some were splintered as though they had been dropped from a great height.

It was a realm of the dead where was but one sign of life. Solomon Kane leaned on his blood-clotted axe and gazed upon the scene with dull, mad eyes. He was grimed and clotted with half-dried blood from long gashes on chest, face, and shoulders, but he paid no heed to his hurts.

The people of Bogonda had not died alone. Seventeen harpies lay among the bones. Six of these Kane had slain. The rest had fallen before the frantic dying desperation of the Bogondi. But it was poor toll to take in return. Of the four hundred-odd people of Upper Bogonda, not one had lived to see the dawn. And the harpies were gone—back to their caves in the black hills, gorged to repletion.

With slow, mechanical steps Kane went about gathering up his weapons. He found his sword, dirk, pistols, and the ju-ju stave. He left the main village and went up the slope to the great hut of Goru. And there he halted, stung by a new horror. The ghastly humor of the harpies had prompted a delicious jest. Above the hut door stared the severed head of Goru. The fat cheeks were shrunken, the lips lolled in an aspect of horrified idiocy, and the eyes stared like a hurt child. And in those dead eyes Kane saw wonder and reproach.

Kane looked at the shambles that had been Bogonda, and he looked at the death mask of Goru. And he lifted his clenched fists above his head, and with glaring eyes raised and writhing lips flecked with froth, he cursed the sky and the earth and the spheres above and below. He cursed the cold stars, the blazing sun, the mocking moon, and the whisper of the wind. He cursed all fates and destinies, all that he had loved or hated, the silent cities beneath the seas, the past ages and the future aeons. In one soul-shaking burst of blasphemy he cursed the gods and devils who make mankind their sport, and he cursed Man who lives blindly on and blindly offers his back to the iron-hoofed feet of his gods.

Then as breath failed he halted, panting. From the lower reaches sounded the deep roaring of a lion and into the eyes of Solomon Kane came a crafty gleam. He stood long, as one frozen, and out of his madness grew a desperate plan. And he silently recanted his blasphemy, for if the brazen-hoofed gods made Man for their sport and plaything, they also gave him a brain that holds craft and cruelty greater than any other living thing.

"There you shall bide," said Solomon Kane to the head of Goru. "The sun will wither you and the cold dews of night will shrivel you. But I will keep the kites from you and your eyes shall see the fall of your slayers. Aye, I could not save the people of Bogonda, but by the God of my race, I can avenge them. Man is the sport and sustenance of titanic beings of Night and Horror whose giant wings hover ever above him. But even evil things may come to an end—and watch ye, Goru."

In the days that followed Kane laboured mightily, beginning with the first grey light of dawn and toiling on past sunset, into the white moonlight till he fell and slept the sleep of utter exhaustion. He snatched food as he worked and he gave his wounds absolutely no heed, scarcely being aware that they healed of themselves. He went down into the lower levels and cut bamboo, great stacks of long, tough stalks. He cut thick branches of trees, and tough vines to serve as ropes.

With this material he reinforced the walls and roof of Goru's hut. He set the bamboos deep in the earth, hard against the wall, and interwove and twined them, binding them fast with the vines that were pliant and tough as cords. The long branches he made fast along the thatch, binding them close together. When he had finished, an elephant could scarcely have burst through the walls.

The lions had come into the plateau in great numbers and the herds of little pigs dwindled fast. Those the lions spared, Kane slew, and tossed to the jackals. This racked Kane's heart, for he was a kindly man and this wholesale slaughter, even of pigs who would fall prey to hunting beasts anyhow, grieved him. But it was part of his plan of vengeance, and he steeled his heart.

The days stretched into weeks. Kane tolled by day and by night, and between his stints he talked to the shrivelled, mummied head of Goru, whose eyes, strangely enough, did not change in the blaze of the sun or the haunt of the moon, but retained their life-like expression. When the memory of those lunacy-haunted days had become only a vague nightmare, Kane wondered if, as it had seemed to him, Goru's dried lips had moved in answer, speaking strange and mysterious things.

Kane saw the akaanas wheeling against the sky at a distance, but they did not come near, even when he slept in the great hut, pistols at hand. They feared his power to deal death with smoke and thunder.

At first he noted that they flew sluggishly, gorged with the flesh they had eaten on that red night, and the bodies they had borne to their caves. But as the weeks passed they appeared leaner and leaner and ranged far afield in search of food. And Kane laughed, deeply and madly.

This plan of his would never have worked before, but now there were no humans to fill the bellies of the harpy-folk. And there were no more pigs. In all the plateau there were no creatures for the bat-people to eat. Why they did not range east of the hills, Kane thought he knew. That must be a region of thick jungle like the country to the west. He saw them fly into the grassland for antelopes and he saw the lions take toll of them. After all, the akaanas were weak beings among the hunters, strong enough only to slay pigs and deer—and humans.

At last they began to soar close to him at night, and he saw their greedy eyes glaring at him through the gloom. He judged the time was ripe. Huge buffaloes, too big and ferocious for the bat-people to slay, had strayed up into the plateau to ravage the deserted fields of the dead Bogondi. Kane out one of these out of the herd and drove him, with shouts and volleys of stones, to the hut of Goru. It was a tedious, dangerous task, and time and again Kane barely escaped the surly bull's sudden charges, but persevered and at last shot the beast before the hut.

A strong west wind was blowing and Kane flung handfuls of blood into the air for the scent to waft to the harpies in the hills. He cut the bull to pieces and carried its quarters into the hut, then managed to drag the huge trunk itself inside. Then he retired into the thick trees nearby and waited.

He had not long to wait. The morning air filled suddenly with the beat of many wings, and a hideous flock alighted before the hut of Goru. All of the beasts—or men—seemed to be there, and Kane gazed in wonder at the tall, strange creatures, so like to humanity and yet so unlike—the veritable demons of priestly legend. They folded their wings like cloaks about them as they walked upright, and they talked to one another in a strident, crackling voice that had nothing of the human in it.

No, Kane decided, these things were not men. They were the materialization of some ghastly jest of Nature—some travesty of the world's infancy when Creation was an experiment. Perhaps they were the offspring of a forbidden and obscene mating of man and beast; more likely they were a freakish offshoot on the branch of evolution—for Kane had long ago dimly sensed a truth in the heretical theories of the ancient philosophers, that Man is but a higher beast. And if Nature made many strange beasts in the past ages, why should she not have experimented with monstrous forms of mankind? Surely Man as Kane knew him was not the first of his breed to walk the earth, nor yet to be the last.

Now the harpies hesitated, with their natural distrust for a building, and some soared to the roof and tore at the thatch. But Kane had builded well. They returned to earth and at last, driven beyond endurance by the smell of raw blood and the sight of the flesh within, one of them ventured inside. In an instant all were crowded into the great hut, tearing ravenously at the meat, and when the last one was within, Kane reached out a hand and jerked a long vine which tripped the catch that held the door he had built. It fell with a crash, and the bar he had fashioned dropped into place. That door would hold against the charge of a wild bull.

Kane came from his cover and scanned the sky. Some hundred and forty harpies had entered the hut. He saw no more winging through the skies and believed it safe to suppose he had the whole flock trapped. Then with a cruel, brooding smile, Kane struck flint and steel to a pile of dead leaves next to the wall. Within sounded an uneasy mumbling as the creatures realized that they were prisoners. A thin wisp of smoke curled upward and a flicker of red followed it; the whole heap burst into flame and the dry bamboo caught.

A few moments later the whole side of the wall was ablaze. The fiends inside scented the smoke and grew restless. Kane heard them cackling wildly and clawing at the walls. He grinned savagely, bleakly and without mirth. Now a veer of the wind drove the flames around the wall and up over the thatch—with a roar the whole hut caught and leaped into flame.

From within sounded a fearful pandemonium. Kane heard bodies crash against the walls, which shook to the impact but held. The horrid screams were music to his soul, and brandishing his arms, he answered them with screams of fearful, soul-shaking laughter. The cataclysm of horror rose unbearably, paling the tumult of the flames. Then it dwindled to a medley of strangled gibbering and gasps as the flames ate in and the smoke thickened. An intolerable scent of burning flesh pervaded the atmosphere, and had there been room in Kane's brain for aught else than insane triumph, he would have shuddered to realize that the scent was of that nauseating and indescribable odour that only human flesh emits when burning.

From the thick cloud of smoke, Kane saw a mewing, gibbering thing emerge through the shredding roof and flap slowly and agonizingly upward on fearfully burned wings. Calmly he aimed and fired, and the scorched and blinded thing tumbled back into the flaming mass just as the walls crashed in. To Kane it seemed that Goru's crumbling face, vanishing in the smoke, split suddenly in a wide grin, and a sudden shout of exultant human laughter mingled eerily in the roar of the flames. But the smoke and insane brain play queer tricks.

Kane stood with the ju-ju stave in one hand and the smoking pistol in the other, above the smouldering ruins that hid forever from the sight of man the last of those terrible, semi-human monsters whom another hero had banished from Europe in an unknown age. Kane stood, an unconscious statue of triumph— the ancient empires fall, the dark-skinned peoples fade and even the demons of antiquity gasp their last, but over all stands the Aryan barbarian, white-skinned, cold-eyed, dominant, the supreme fighting man of the earth, whether he be clad in wolf-hide and horned helmet, or boots and doublet—whether he bear in his hand battle-ax or rapier—whether he be called Dorian, Saxon or Englishman—whether his name is Jason, Hengist or Solomon Kane.

Smoke curled upward into the morning sky, and the roaring of foraging lions shook the plateau. Slowly, like light breaking through mists, sanity returned to him.

"The light of God's morning enters even into dark and lonesome lands," said Solomon Kane sombrely. "Evil rules in the waste lands of the earth, but even evil may come to an end. Dawn follows midnight and even in this lost land the shadows shrink. Strange are Thy ways, oh God of my people, and who am I to question Thy wisdom? My feet have fallen in evil ways but Thou hast brought me forth scatheless and hast made me a scourge for the Powers of Evil. Over the souls of men spread the condor wings of colossal monsters and all manner of evil things prey upon the heart and soul and body of Man. Yet it may be in some far day the shadows shall fade and the Prince of Darkness be chained forever in his hell. And till then mankind can but stand up stoutly to the monsters in his own heart and without, and with the aid of God he may yet triumph."

And Solomon Kane looked up into the silent hills and felt the silent call of the hills and the unguessed distances beyond; and Solomon Kane shifted his belt, took his staff firmly in his hand and turned his face eastward.

THE END

Made in the USA
Coppell, TX
05 April 2024

30940103R00111